Ladies

Of

Tunica

By
Dee Alessandra

Ideas come from all corners. This one came from Hank Cashman, author, poker analyst and columnist, dealer and observer of poker players. There is no one on this planet who knows more about poker strategy than Hank. I am in his debt for the expertise he provided.

Thanks also to Levi Garcia, Dylan Scott and Mary Smith for their technical assistance.

This book is a work of fiction and any similarities to persons, places or events is purely coincidental.

Based on the 2007 Writers' Digest Award winning short story of the same title.

Copyright 2010
ISBN: 1453825185

Published in the United States of America:

Chapter 1

Margaret Youngman entered the empty elevator, spun her blocky frame around and pressed number 7. She was wiped out from the strain of the long hours at the poker table, but she was exhilarated, too, because she was officially in the top sixteen, a money win, and now she'd earn more than the thousand it cost to be in the tournament. She made a mental note to return the money to Jay Gerson, the man who was financially responsible for her being here in Tunica in the first place. Her smile widened.

The elevator door was sliding shut. A hand reached in to pull the doors back open. Greg Guyler stood close to her, his dark eyes shiny in the mirrored car. He turned to her as the doors slid shut.

She stepped back to make room for the familiar figure, recognizing him from the tables. Looking sideways, she was aware of their reflections receding over and over, trapped in the seeming endless space of mirrors.

"You made sixteen, right?" He turned his bulky body and pointed the neck of his beer bottle at her.

"I did. I never thought I'd make it but I guess my luck held out. How did you do? Are you still in the running?" She noticed that he hadn't pressed a floor button. The elevator was still.

He hiked up his shoulders, shifted his beer bottle to the other hand and burped loudly. Margaret flinched. As he spoke she couldn't help but notice his small yellow teeth. Inside, she pictured herself probing beneath his gums for the certain build-up of gray plaque, the bleeding of over-sensitive gums and discovering the revealing wince from the tooth that needed a root canal. She mentally backed away from her professional dental tech meanderings to Greg Guyler's questioning eyes.

"I didn't make it yet, but I will. Oh, yeah, I will. But you won't, get my drift?" She noticed his tight lips formed a perfect 'v' above his chubby chin.

"I don't understand."

"Don't be dumb. Go home. Get a makeover or something. Just take your dough and stop winning. What are you doing here anyways? You got nothin' better to do? No boyfriend? No hubby, kids? You need to just go home."

He burped again, this time holding the bottle to his lips as he pointed a finger at her. "Ladies shouldn't be playing poker. It's for guys. Guys who drink beer and know how to play the game, that's who it's for. What do you know about bluffing and betting and when to fold and when to hold? Better listen up, lady."

"Or? Are you threatening me?" Her cheeks were red, spotted with white. She pushed her head back, chin out, knowing that she shouldn't be intimidated by someone like Greg Guyler, a no-class, beer drinking, second-rate poker player. Holding his gaze with hers, she saw the flinch, the slight look away and she knew that he was the one who felt intimidated. If he was any good, really a pure poker player, he wouldn't feel the need to say what he was saying.

He hit the 'open door' button. "You don't know me or what I'm capable of. No broad is going to win this tournament. Not while I'm in the game, and I am in the game to stay. You hear me? I'm in this tournament for the long haul and don't you forget it. And no mealy-mouthed little girl is going to win it or you'll be sorry. Tell your little giggly friends I said so."

As he stepped out, she said to him softly, "Is that right? Well look who is at a money table and who is not. Hello, it's a girl."

He turned to her quickly. Maggie flinched and took a step backward She rued having antagonized him and hoped he would not step back into the elevator. He did not. He stared at her coldly as the doors slid shut with a hiss.

Again she was alone in the elevator, watching herself disappear into the depths of the mirrored walls, over and over, dimmer and dimmer. Her image repeated itself until she could no longer see the last figure. It became lost in obscurity. The car rocked gently on its way up to the seventh floor, Margaret in deep thought remembering the stares from Guyler, the slitted eyes, the tight lips, the quick sips of beer. Now she knew why. He despised females at the table. If he lost to a lady it would make him feel impotent. Could he be gay like Max, the trucker, who was also filled with hate? She didn't really think so; he seemed more driven by winning this tournament at all costs and especially didn't want to lose to a woman. Margaret contemplated this thought. He has been around poker for many years, probably, and it was old school poker, a male game. Also, she was sure he was here not just to win but to prove to someone that he could do it. She smiled as her nerves settled a bit, convinced that she had this man's threat figured out. He was a screw-up out to vindicate himself by eliminating the roadblocks on his highway to a successful tournament. She'd have to ask the other ladies if he touched base with them, too. He must be making the rounds of the women, she figured.

Chapter 2

She was not homely, Margaret was just plain. At nineteen she had finished high school with all its social heartache, and now faced classes at the community college. Her daddy read the brochure and advised her to take courses in dental hygiene.

She pictured herself in a white uniform and white, foam-soled shoes, taking full charge of the patient in front of her. She felt empowered, respected, even a little fearful because she was able, if she liked, to inflict pain. A licensed dental hygienist the brochure stated. She smiled at the vision, eyes shining as she looked at her dad.

"That way you'll be able to study faces up real close with no one the wiser. It's perfect, Maggie. You'll be a real poker pro. It took me thirty years to figure out all the tics and twitches and what they mean. You'll learn it all in a third of that time by pokin' round folk's mugs all day. It's a dream profession, missy and I hear it pays pretty dang well, too. What do you think, Gert?"

Margaret's mom was a lean, short woman with jet black short, straight hair that she wore tucked behind her ears. High cheekbones and gleaming dark eyes gave her face the severity of an Apache. She glanced at Herb Youngman.

"If you think we can afford it and if it's what Maggie wants, then I suppose it's a good idea. But as I said, it has to be what the child wants and in the middle of it all we can't just up and tell her there's no more money. Know what I'm sayin'? I'm sure it's going to take a good, three or four thousand a year for the two years. We can do it now, but what about the snags that might come along? Don't get me wrong. I'm all for it, but...." Her voice faded, unsure.

"Hell, Honey. Where we going with the money? Banking it isn't enjoyin' it and all we do is bank it. Business is good. Who would ever think that Clay County had the potential to grow this way? The foundations that need to be laid in all these sub-divisions and factories give me all the work I need. Hell, I don't even kill myself these days. All I do is order materials and supervise the concrete guys. And the money is just fine. You go sign up, Mag."

"Daddy, are you sure? I could get a job at the uniform factory."

"Yeah, right," Herb snorted. "No, you go to school some more. I have a good feeling about this. Not the cleaning choppers part, the faces, you know."

Gert giggled. "Your daddy wants you to be one of those millionaire poker players, get on the television and bring him a bucket of bills. Herb, let me tell you something, you think you're such a hot shot poker face reader, but we've been married a lot of years and you never know what I'm thinking."

"I know. I just choose not to react to your evil thoughts. Bet you're the witchiest woman in Birchwood, West Virginia." He laughed out loud, sipped his coffee and ran his hand through his blonde messy hair and along his scruffy beard. "Just don't go putting any spells on us. You always think the worst is going to happen. Think nice thoughts for a change."

Maggie felt good. She loved her parents' banter. Gert had a sharp tongue that kept Herb on his toes and in her eyes, Maggie was a perfect child who could do no wrong. Gert felt in her heart that if her Maggie was ever faced with the temptation to do something immoral or illegal, she just wouldn't do it. She supported her little one all through high school, the clubs, the band practices, all the miserable dances, bake sales and whatever else it took to get it all in the past. Maggie was never popular, she was plain. Her hair was a mousy brown, her blue eyes always seemed pale and lost in her round face. Though her complexion was fair, she blushed too easily. Food was her bane. Gert was an excellent cook, strictly southern style. She was heavy on the fats, bacon, biscuits with gravy and sweet tea. Maggie was always plump by at least twenty pounds.

She stood to go upstairs. Tomorrow she'd register for classes and have to buy some books.

"Will you have a check for me tomorrow, then? And one for books, too?"

"Don't worry about it. After supper you want to go to Ray's? Two truckers from Richmond heard about his games and they'll layover in that back parking lot. Be fun to play with new faces, right?" He emptied the last of the coffee and looked at her questioningly.

"Sure. But I'll need to leave early to get to Birchwood Community College registration by 7 a.m. I don't want to spend all day there in long lines." She hesitated, her hands holding the back of the chair.

"What?"

Gert gazed at Maggie as she spoke to Herb. "What's the matter, Herb? You can't read that open face? Here it is in a nutshell. Correct me if I'm wrong, Margaret, but you always give your winnings to Daddy. But now things are about to change. Now you want a loan, a stake from him is all. But you'll return the stake, only the stake. You want to keep your winnings, buy your own books, make your own deposits, then, after a few serious games behind Ray's Barber Shop, you'd like to pay for your own courses." She slapped her hand on the vinyl flowered tablecloth. "Can I read faces, or what?"

Herb looked stunned. Maggie always turned over the winnings to him at the end of a poker session. Oh, he'd give her a few dollars for school stuff, but it was tradition with him. He was her father and took her to games to learn.

"Is that how you want to do it, Baby?"

"Daddy, that's exactly how I'd like to do it. Mom, you're good. Want to join us?"

Gert tucked a stray strand of hair behind her ear. "No. I might get addicted to poker like you two. Then who'd get supper? No thanks."

After Maggie went upstairs, Gert turned to her husband, a sharp crease between her brows.

"We're okay with this, then? The school, all the stuff she'll need, you know."

"Yeah, I know. We are more than okay, Gert, honest. I meant it when I said business was good. You remember that industrial park up in Farber County?"

She smiled. "All the way over in the next county? You boys are really spreading yourselves thin, aren't you? You'll have to leave for work in the dark and come home in the dark." She shook her head.

"Nah. It's not that far. It's this side of the highway. You've been there, to the apple place, remember? It's only about forty minutes tops. Two new buildings going up there and we got the bid. It's a big job and the money will put us way ahead. Then all the sub-divisions around here are real bread and butter jobs. It doesn't show signs of slowing up, either."

"I know I worry a lot, especially about the money. But one of us has to. Mostly I worry you'll gamble it all away, but I know in my heart of hearts that you have control. Teach that to Maggie, will you? She loves to play poker as much as you do and when you encourage her the way you do it really makes me worry. Some nights I can't sleep.

"No more worrying, Hon. The cards are for fun and you know I only take what I can afford. Usually, I bring home more than I take, so where's the reason to worry? I have all bases covered, believe it. Maggie will be all right. Hell, she's smarter than her old man when it comes to cards. She'll get real serious about her poker. For me, the cards are just for fun and the little extra money is there to mess with like trips to your sister, a new car once in a while, like that. Okay?"

She snuggled against his chest as he wrapped his arms around her warmly."Now how about that supper you were talking about"?

Chapter 3

Ray dealt the first hand to the nine players around the table in the back room of the barber shop. Maggie liked the smell of shaving cream and lotion. She settled in the chair next to Herb and watched Ray, the barber expertly shuffle and deal the cards.

"Walter, you bring chips?" Ray asked the local butcher, a skinny, hollow-cheeked man who giggled at all his hands driving the table to make many an unwise bet.

"Yeah, I sure did." He poured the chips into the bowl and passed them around. "I had to wrestle them away from the little woman." His shrill laugh was contagious.

"Little?" Ray shot up an eyebrow. "That's not really the right word, Walter."

"You're so right. But, there's more to love, right, Margaret?"

Blushing wildly, Maggie couldn't help but smile despite her struggle to hold it in.

Steve from the hardware store had a few six packs and Marty from the uniform factory placed a bag of pretzels on the corner of the table.

Herb pushed a can of soda over to Maggie. "One vice in the family is enough." He stared at his two cards, a pair of kings.

The two truckers stayed in with junk, Maggie had two tens and folded deciding to wait a few hands. Everyone else folded. The flop was an Ace, a three and a jack. Herb raised and the truckers stayed. The street card was another three. Herb raised again. The truckers folded and Herb took the pot.

As the evening progressed, one by one the regulars dropped out. Maggie had a hunch some of them called it a night when the treats were gone.

"I'll get you guys next time," whined the butcher as he shrugged on his jacket and headed for the back door.

Maggie took a small pot, a hundred and eighty dollars, from one of the truckers.

"You should be ashamed a yerself, Max," his partner laughed good-naturedly, "to have a gal beat up on you so bad."

Max wasn't smiling as he stared across the table at Maggie. She avoided his beady eyes under the dark baseball cap. Silently, she stacked her chips.

"I can only play for about another half hour. Just so you all know. I have school and shopping to do early tomorrow morning."

"Deal, then, Ray. My daughter's a college student now, so let me see if I can get some of my dough back to help pay for her studying."

Max ground out a cigarette. "Looks like she's doin' okay all by herself, fer a girl, that is. Nice pile you got there, sweetheart."

Ray flipped the cards. Maggie caught a king, ten and decided to fold, to lay back a little more, then pounce, the way her daddy taught her.

Max bluffed into a big pot and lost, stoking his anger once again. Herb coughed and glanced over at Maggie.

"You'd best get going there, young lady. Big day for you tomorrow."

"Just a few more hands, Dad. I'd like to see if my luck changes. I've been getting too many low cards."

She folded her next hand, then bet twenty dollars on a queen, jack of diamonds. Max the trucker held an Ace, nine off suit. By now he was totally frustrated by Maggie's style which he just could not read. He went over her twenty and raised the pot by eighty dollars. Herb threw in a hundred, as did Ray. They both had bluff hands.

The flop gave Maggie a jack, ten off suit, pairing her jack. All four players checked. The street card was nine, making Max throw in another eighty dollars. The other two folded and Maggie went all in. Max called. He looked over at Maggie's two jacks and cursed under his breath.

"C'mon, Ray. I need the river. Give me a nine or an ace, c'mon. Save my ass here, will you?"

Ray pushed a face down card to one side and flipped over the river card, a deuce of hearts.

Max threw his cards across the table. "Dammit."

Maggie scooped up her winnings, well over three hundred dollars, and stood up.

"That's it for me. I need to go."

Max glared and said angrily, "What, no chance to win my money back?"

"Hold on, there, fella. Maggie warned everyone she had to leave early. It's fair and square, winning or losing."

The other trucker stood, too. "Let's go, Max. We have a run to finish. Good game, folks. It was interestin' all the way. Herb, you ought to consider putting your daughter in a tournament or two, you know, for the experience. She's good, hard to read and real cool for a girl."

"That's always been the idea, boys."

"Yeah, tell me about it," Max grumbled as he pulled on his light tan leather jacket.

Maggie started for the door.

"Hold up, Maggie. I'll be right with you." Herb shoved a few bills into his wallet and watched as the two truckers left.

Ray smiled towards Maggie. "Honey, why don't you wait until we hear those trucks leave, okay?"

"Why? Do you think…."

"Never know. We don't know those boys and that Max was really pissed."

Herb went to the window as the trucks pulled out, a short pull on their horns to say bye.

"Oh, they'll get over it. They didn't lose that much. See, they're gone." Maggie went out the door, Herb following.

"Night, Ray."

"Night, Herb. Say, there is a tourney every Thursday in Elmwood. Be good for Maggie to give it a shot. It costs a hundred and the last five collect. They divvy up the purse. You should take her once in a while. She could make some real school money. Sammy the butcher went two weeks ago and came in fourth, for a winning of three hundred and fifty dollars. First place cleared two thousand."

"Two thousand?" Herb whistled softly.

"Yessir. Even if she comes in fifth, she'll double her money. Nothing to sneeze at, eh?"

"Sounds good. Thanks for the tip. See you next Thursday. Be careful of the visitors, okay?"

The scream was piercing. Ray knocked his chair backwards as he ran out the door behind Herb. The last two players ran out to the back porch, too. Maggie was frozen on the side of the driveway next to the barber shop. Both her hands were up to her cheeks in fright, her eyes wide in the bright light of the oncoming truck. Max hit the brakes and the load bounced and screeched to a halt. He shouted out the window.

"Forgot something. Now I'm runnin' late. Didn't see you there, young lady. Be more careful. See you guys around."

He pulled the horn once again as he sped out of the driveway. Herb ran to Maggie's side.

"What happened?"

"I was just walking to the car when he barreled down the driveway. He....he came so close. I thought, I was sure he wanted to hit me. I guess he went around the building and made another pass. I didn't know what to do." Her cheeks were crimson.

"Let's go home."

Ray put his hand on her shoulder. "Now don't you go letting the likes of that punk get the best of you. He's a big nothing and worse than that, he's a poor loser. Never be intimidated by that type."

****

Four trips to Elmwood gave Maggie a third, fourth, first and out of the money experiences. She had three thousand in the bank, kept up with her tuition payments and, at the urging of her study friend, Jean, she now sported platinum blonde highlights and clothes that were slimming and flattering.

"You need to wear longer tops to give you a lean look. And get some of that eye make-up. It'll help you look wide eyed and wonderful." Jean sparkled when she spoke. Maggie hung on every word and followed all of Jean's tips, even those on eating habits. "You don't have to eat everything your mom makes, or if you do, take small plates. That stuff will kill you eventually."

At the end of the first school year, not only was Maggie at the head of the class, she looked like a new girl, confident, upbeat and sure of her future.

Then Herb had his heart attack. Everyone agreed that he was so brave to pull over to the side of the road, slump over the wheel and die peacefully. That's how the EMT's found him after a 911 call from a passing motorist. Gert and Maggie received the call from the police on a sunny October afternoon while they prepared dinner and waited for Herb to come home from the big job in the industrial park.

Herb Youngman's wake was the talk of Birchwood. The funeral parlor was filled with floral arrangements the likes of which the residents of Birchwood had never seen. Maggie smiled as she watched family and friends point appreciatively at an easel holding a straight of hearts all done in dyed mums, or the poker chip creation of rose buds and the University of West Virginia thoroughbred made of roses and dried coneflowers. The crowd from Ray's Barber Shop chipped in for a pair of dice done in tight mums. She knew Daddy would have loved it, squeezed Gert's hand and smiled through her tears.

Later, over coffee in the small kitchen, Gert spoke softly.

"Your father was a smart man, Maggie. I didn't know that he took out an insurance policy on himself separate from the one we both had. I don't even know when he did it. He just went to the office and took out the policy on his own. Now we have two policies and my bank account is bulging. What about that?"

"That's okay, I guess. But I'd rather have Daddy. He'll never see me graduate or get the job he always said would pay 'dang well.' Remember that?"

She smiled sadly. "Yes, I remember the hopes he had for you. I do, too. Some day you'll be in one of those big tournaments he always talked about and believe me, he will be there at your side cheering you on."

Chapter 4

With mask in place, Maggie meticulously maneuvered the stainless steel pick in and out of Barry Orman's teeth, a nice mix of his own and a few implants. Barry's face was immobile despite Maggie's occasional harder than necessary probes. She smiled behind her mask.

"Do you play cards, Mr. Orman?"

She leaned back as he rinsed his mouth in the little swirling sink and wiped with the paper bib around his neck.

"Not too much. I like the black jack at the casino, but that's about it. Why?"

She unhooked his bib, removed and tossed her mask and gloves into the garbage. Her hair hung loosely over her shoulders as she jotted information on his chart.

"Because you have the perfect poker face. It's very difficult to figure out what you're thinking. Like when I'm cleaning your teeth, you don't move a muscle in your face even when I know you should."

"You mean you're hurting me on purpose? Just to get a rise out of me?" He pushed himself up off the chair.

"Oh, no. I wouldn't do that. It's just that there are sensitive areas and it's impossible to avoid them when I'm doing a thorough cleaning." She walked with him to the door.

"Well, it doesn't matter. I don't play poker anyway. None of my pals play, so I guess I'll stick to the black jack when I get to the casino."

She blushed but kept her eyes on his. "I'd like to teach you. I think you'd make an excellent player."

"You mean like an experiment? Do you play poker? Wait, that's a silly question. How can you teach me if you don't know how to play? Are you any good at it?"

"Well, yes. I've been playing all of my life. I've played tournaments all over the state, and thanks to poker, my education was a gift. I admit, Mr. Orman, I still have a lot to learn, but I believe I can teach you a whole lot."

"Please, call me Barry. I have an idea that might please you. Do you know where O'Hara's restaurant and lounge is in Harrison?"

"The one that used to be Gary's, on the river? I heard that place was sold. So now it's O'Hara's?" Maggie sat at the reception desk, placing Barry's folder in the wire basket. "That's not too far from where I live."

"After college, one of my buddies decided to go to the culinary institute instead of getting his MBA. He just bought the place. He told me that there's a game in the back room once in a while and if I tell my friend that we want to play, he'll be sure to set it up. Saturday night around nine be okay with you?"

"Fine, then. I'll meet you there. Be prepared to lose some money. Remember, I know your face well, every nook and tic." She smiled smugly, her cheeks high with the blush of pink.

As he went out the door he said softly, "I'm really scared but some of my pals will be there and I think they'll give you a run for that money."

****

O'Hara's was a mid-scale sports bar, lounge and family restaurant. Evidently Barry's friend not only had business sense, but he was creative as well. Maggie admired the art work, florals for the ladies, hunting scenes for the gents.

He picked up his glass of wine and pointed it at her. "To the gentlest dental hygienist in the county."

"Even though I hurt you?"

"You didn't even come close. I have a high pain threshold. Here comes Tim O'Hara."

A lanky young man with black hair and crystal blue eyes folded himself into the booth next to Barry.

"Did you folks order? What do you like? May I suggest the broccoli cheddar soup, chicken strips in Marsalis wine, then the medallions of veal in a light béarnaise sauce, topped with shitake mushrooms and broiled asparagus? On me, of course."

"You describe the food like a fag, you know." Barry wiggled the menu at his friend.

"I am a fag, remember?"

Barry laughed. "You actually do make me forget once in a while. The part about the meal being on you sounded good though. By the way, this is my new friend, Maggie Youngman. Maggie, meet my college pal, Tim O'Hara, owner of this fine establishment and the richest fag I know."

Maggie reached over the table to shake Tim's hand. It was a soft, comforting hand and he held onto hers warmly, placing his other on top.

"Any friend of Barry's. I understand you like a friendly game? After dinner we'll go to my office. I've invited three others to join us." He looked over at Barry. "Remember Rini She's in Elmwood for three days on business, so she and her new hubby will be here."

Barry leaned toward Maggie. "Rini graduated at the top of our class. She's a patent attorney in Cincinnati. The only business she'd have in Elmwood is with a client who just came up with a new style of computer chip."

Tim placed both hands on the table in front of him. "And get this, her husband is CEO of the Star Rose Casino in Cincinnati. They are rolling in dough."

"Well, we always knew she'd be most likely to succeed. Be nice to see her again. Who's the third player?"

"One of our suppliers. He delivers our paper goods and stays for a game with us on occasion. He's pretty rough around the edges but a sharp card player. Rini will be a challenge, too. How about you, Maggie?"

"I hold my own in tournaments, if that's any endorsement. I did have an excellent teacher, too. Mostly I just enjoy the game and the different styles of play."

Tim O'Hara's office was not only spacious, he had state of the art appliances installed down one wall of counters and overhead cupboards. He removed a linen tablecloth from a corner table revealing a highly polished top. The six players sat around leisurely sipping their drinks.

Tim tore the cellophane off a deck of cards.
"We're just like the pros, eh?"
Rini Gerson and her husband, Jay smiled at Maggie.
"We're the Gersons, Rini and Jay." She settled into her chair. Maggie noticed her wrist watch, a lady Rolex and a lustrous double strand of black pearls against a soft pink cashmere pullover. Maggie felt plain even with highlights in her hair. Rini's flaming red curls lit up the table. In contrast, Jay Gerson appeared tired, pale, a once-handsome blonde man who now appeared to need a vacation. The look may have been deceiving though, because the hand he extended to Maggie was firm confident, and, his deep blue eyes were as sharp as a hawk.
"I'm Maggie Youngman. I understand you run a casino. What an exciting profession."
"It is. You have no idea what goes on behind the scenes. What do you do, young lady?"
"Nothing too dramatic. I'm a dental technician. I'm probably one of the few who really likes the job, though."
"Finally, here's our sixth player. Folks, this is Max, one of our delivery men. Max you'll get to know everyone as we go along." Tim began dealing.
Maggie's throat tightened. She looked down at her cards, her cheeks flushed. Barry leaned close to her.
"You all right?"
She kept her head down seemingly overly intense about a jack of hearts and a five of spades. She folded, avoiding a glance at Max.

He bet twenty on an Ace of hearts and jack of clubs. Barry had two tens and saw Max's twenty. Rini bet, Tim and Jay folded. The flop was a three of spades and a six, seven of hearts. Rini was holding a four and five of hearts. She had the straight. Max raised the bet to forty, everyone stayed. The street card was an Ace of diamonds. Max raised the bet to sixty. Barry folded, afraid Max might be holding an Ace. The river was the nine of clubs. Max called and turned over his two Aces. Rini smiled widely.

"Straight," she said triumphantly, scooping in the money.

Maggie didn't smile. She knew Max was fuming behind his stoic stare.

Three hands later, after slow playing her cards, Maggie drew a pair of Aces. She bet twenty, Max bet as did Jay and Tim.

The flop gave her a king, jack and ten, but Jay now had a pair of tens, Tim had a nine and six of diamonds. Max stared at the flop. He held a jack, seven and felt his pair of jacks would hold. He raised the bet to sixty. Maggie pushed her money in, about four hundred dollars. Tim quickly folded, and after some thoughtful staring, Jay gently pushed his cards, face down to the side. Max looked over at Maggie, straggly strands of thin brown hair curling around his ears, poking out of his black ball cap. His eyes were shaded, but Maggie could feel them burning into hers. Did he finally recognize her as the mousy teenager from the back room of Ray's barber shop? She could feel a line of perspiration beading on her upper lip.

"I call." He turned over his cards. Maggie looked over at his pair of jacks. Slowly, she turned over her Aces. Max hit the table in disgust. "Damn women," he muttered as Tim flipped over the river card, a third Ace for Maggie. "Look at that. She ends up with trip Aces adding insult to injury. Can you believe it?"

"It's poker, Max." Tim stood and stretched his lanky frame against a grey silk suit. "That's the way it goes, folks. I need to close up shop here in twenty minutes." Tim retrieved the money box from the counter. "Change your chips back into dough and we'll do it again next time. I can hardly wait, Barry. It was interesting all right."

Outside, Barry and Jay shook hands, he hugged Rini tightly making her right leg lift in classic Class B movie style. Maggie giggled at the sight.

"Don't be strangers now, you two."

"You, too, Sweetie," Rini said. "Now you have a poker buddy, start traveling around. You're always welcome to our place in Cincinnati, right Jay?"

"Of course. Maggie, I was so impressed by your style of play. A friend of mine owns a Casino in Tunica. He runs a nice open tournament there every once in a while. Here, take my card." He wrote on the back then handed it to her. "Give this to him and you're in. He'll wave the fee and comp you a room and meals, too. He'll treat you fine. I guarantee, once you go you'll become a regular."

"I never thought of entering a real big formal tournament. But Tunica sounds nice. Maybe I will."

Thanks. It was so nice meeting you both. I enjoyed our little game."
"Barry, you watch this one. You'll learn a lot from her. Here's a player who knows how to use the table. She's a reader. Listen to her, you hear?" Rini wagged her long cultured finger at him.
Jay put his arm around his wife. "I thought my Rini was good at a table, and she is, but you have a special gift, little lady. It was a pleasure to watch you read our faces. You're lucky, Barry, to have such a delightful friend."
They walked slowly down the sidewalk to the parking lot. Huge moths fluttered against the pole lights along the way. Maggie felt euphoric. She had just won over eight hundred dollars, Max didn't recognize her, she beat him again and she walked on the arm of the most handsome man she knew.
"What are you smiling about? You're looking pretty smug." Barry turned left out of O'Hara's, the setting sun flooding the car in golden rays.
"Oh, nothing too much. I had fun, your friends are cool and the game was, well, interesting. Where are we going by the way?"
"I'll get you back to your car in just a few minutes. There's some spot I want to share with you."
She blushed. "I know just about every place around Clay County. How far is it?"
"Not far. Be patient. Yes, my friends are okay for the most part. Except for Max. The guy carries a serious chip on his shoulder."

"Why is that? I think he's just an angry man, you know, intimidating. I sat at a poker table with him once before, with my Daddy at the barber shop. He was such a poor loser."

Barry was quiet as he drove. He seemed distracted. "I don't think you really read everyone at the table tonight."

"What do you mean? You were perfectly obvious about Tim's tendencies. Rini and Jay are content with each other, you're you and Max is, well, he's a Max. What did I miss?"

He turned off the main road, down a narrow lane to where the trees stopped and the lane went through a meadow on top of a high rise. The view was unobstructed by trees, and, Maggie noticed, there was no guardrail. Below, the lights of Birchwood, the highway, the river traffic reflecting off the still waters took Maggie's breath away.

"How did you find this place? It's magical and it's so close to everything. It's an ideal spot for a home. This edge needs a guard rail, though. I love it. You're incredible, Barry."

He leaned his head back. I once thought I might build here, but things in my life changed. Now, I just come here on occasion to relax. Maybe I should have explained earlier. Tim's just getting over a breakup with a media consultant from a major TV affiliate in Wheeling. That's why he re-located and bought the restaurant. He also had a thing with Max, but that didn't work out and they both had a difficult time for a while. Max had been living with another trucker for years and when it fell apart, he met Tim. They've both been on an emotional roller coaster."

Maggie leaned back against the seat. "Another trucker? Max? This is so unreal."

He laughed. You should know about Miss Rini, too. Jay is her third hubby. The first two were also well along in years and very rich. Our 'Most Likely to Succeed' really has succeeded. The gal is worth millions through no fault of her own. She's just had lucky marriages."

"You don't think…."

"Nah. There was some talk but Rini couldn't have been that feral."

Maggie shook her head. "I should be so lucky. You should be a little older."

He sighed. "Or richer, or straighter."

Silence.

"I have never been more comfortable with a girl than I have been with you, Maggie Youngman. I like to talk with you, I like your laugh, you have so much class."

She glanced sideways at him. "But I'm not your type, right?"

"You are definitely someone's type and I hate him, you know. I'm sorry. I should have been up front with you. Can we still be friends?"

Punching him lightly in the shoulder, she leaned against him. "As if I'd ever let you go. Take me to my car now, okay? It has been one wild night."

They rode along silently.

"Uh, you and Max?"

"Definitely not my type."
"Thank God."

****

The house was quiet. Maggie saw the blue, orange, and green flashes of the TV coming from the back room. Her mom was waiting up, again.

"Mom. I'm home. Be right there. Want anything from the kitchen?"

"No, I'm all right."

Maggie came into the little room that was, by far, the room used most by them ever since Herb put on the addition three years ago. Maggie sat in an overstuffed chair, put up her feet and sipped a cola.

"Nice date, Honey?" Gert was wrapped in an oversized, floral fleece robe.

"You shouldn't wait up for me, Mom. I am a big girl now. My date? Let's see. He was handsome, mannerly, rich, a computer wizard, in short, the kind of guy you've been praying I'd find, right?" Maggie grinned at her wide-eyed mother.

"So?"

"So, he's gay."

"Oh, my. You poor baby."

"Ah, what the heck. I found a good friend anyway. He really is all those things I said, though" She stared at the TV, her mind drifting back to the depressing events of the evening.

"Aunt Libby wants us to move in with her. I really want to, Maggie. Since your Daddy died, and you started to work, I spend all my time sitting around here doing nada." Gert folded her robed arms around herself.

"What about me? I'm not going to rattle around here all by myself."

Maggie loved her Aunt Libby, her big old house in Bristol, Virginia, but most of all, she knew how happy it made her mother just to spend time with her older sister. Now that Libby's husband was in a nursing home suffering from Alzheimer's disease, she, too, was alone. It made sense, Maggie knew.

"As Daddy always used to say, 'It's a smart financial move, so do it.' So let's do it. I can be a dental technician anywhere."

Gert's face brightened, her eyes shone. "You mean it? I was so worried. We can sell the house and move? You won't be sorry. We can travel to new places. The change will be good for us. You'll see."

"I know, Mom. We'll be fine. Let's call the real estate office first thing in the morning."

Chapter 5

Northern Broadway in Westchester County, New York City is a world away from the glitter and glamour of Times Square. Blocks of neat cape cods, ranches, mini-estates and gated communities mix comfortably with small businesses and nicely landscaped office complexes.
At the end of one lushly treed driveway at the northernmost end of the county, the Guyler's stone and brick home sat surrounded by clipped hedges, manicured lawns and flower beds sporting concrete statuary. Olivia Guyler collected statues like other ladies in the neighborhood collected Depression glass or ceramic teapots. Her taste was part classical, part whimsical, so there were Greek and Roman style ladies draped in off-the- shoulder creased dresses, grazing deer and herons, gnomes, even two flamingos. Fortunately, the grounds were large enough to balance it all in the many areas of shrubs, trees and flowers.
On the brick steps leading to the wide double oak doors, Greg Guyler sulked in the hot sun, short thick black hair gleaming, his lip in a sneer as he thought about his baby sister who turned eighteen yesterday and was now slowly driving her new yellow Mustang along the side of the house. She waved at her brother from behind the wheel of her birthday present. When he was eighteen three years ago, his gift was a check for a thousand dollars.
"There you go, Greg," his father said. "That's a good start toward a car. Save up."

He scrunched his round race into classic disappointment. "But, Dad, Eugene got a GMC. This is not fair at all."

His father hiked up his trousers, ran his fingers through his wiry black and white hair and shifted his ragged cigar from one side of his mouth to the other.

"Eugene works hard at the business. He learned it all by himself. He's smart. He can lay tile, wall-to-wall, hardwood, all of it. He needs a vehicle for the business. If you'd get your head out of your ass you'd be out of school by now and workin' with your brother. But you'd rather fool around, flunk courses, screw up. Be more like your brother, kid. You don't see him behind the deli playing poker all hours of the night. One of these days you'll end up in jail, and believe me when I tell you this, do not call me because I will not go to no jail to pick you up at no three a.m. I hope you understand that. Just because you're eighteen doesn't mean you're grown up. You understand?"

"Right, Dad. Eugene does okay in the business because you're the boss and you know I'm right. He's so boring he could never work for anyone else. He's the biggest kiss-ass I know. Good thing he met a boring girl in high school and got married otherwise he'd be living with you forever. He could never do anything but lay tile, I bet."

"Don't be a smart-ass. Flooring is a good business. People always need rugs and tiles. Lots of building goin' on around here, too. Shit, I'm thinkin' of opening another store up in Rye."

Greg scoffed. "Who's going to run it for you? Eugene the Giant?"

"For your information, your brother is starting school to get a degree in business, so yeah, sure, he can run it, and he'll be able to do a bang-up job too. There's something you can put your money on, big shot. Play your cards right and he might put you in charge of, let's say, the hardwood flooring section."

"No way could I work for big bro. Let me just stay on here in Westchester where I know everyone. Plus, I can bring in some business, like I did last week."

Frank scoffed. "Oh, yes. The recliner and the leather sofa over in Queens. I just hope their check doesn't bounce. Those two looked pretty shady to me. Their kid is one of your poker buds, right?"

"He is and don't worry. Tiny's parents are good for it. They both work for the transit."

"Whatever."

"What do you mean, whatever? His folks are very nice and they like me, too. When I visit Tiny, his parents treat me like I'm special."

"So, go live with Tiny's parents. Maybe they can straighten you out so you don't have to live here forever."

"It won't be forever. I just need to save a little more money so I can find a place that I like."

Frank Guyler scoffed. "Your mother makes it too easy for you here. She does too much for you. Get a little more independent, do things for yourself, for Christ's sake. You're such a leech."

"I do my share. You just refuse to notice."

Chapter 6

"How did you know I was bluffin' again?" Greg stared across the kitchen counter at his classmate and poker nemesis, Nina Krepelli. "Your eyes again. They kind of quiver from side to side when you know you got nothing and you should throw in but you're too stubborn to do that even if you know it's right." She shook the chestnut hair out of her eyes and glared at him. "You're so easy to read, Guyler. So easy."

"Yeah. Only for you. I guess guys don't spend so much time lookin' at other guys' eyes. That's why I'm usually such a big winner when I play at the Saturday nights." He shuffled the cards expertly. Nina sighed inwardly. She liked Greg, a lot, but it depressed her because he had so many faults, like a sour disposition, a forever angry expression and a real badass attitude about everything. All of these aspects of his character she knew, in her heart of hearts, she could never change. But, to her, there was an element of surprise when he'd look at her and try to suppress a smile, or maybe it was a smirk, and a few times he even gave her a meaningless wink. She knew she was kidding herself and wasting her time, but still….

"What makes you so mean, Guyler?" She dug in her little yellow purse and pulled out a stick of gum which she popped into her mouth after tossing the foil wrap at him. "Family? Friends? What friends? Your weight, your lack of poker skill, what? You always have a puss on, those eyes of yours are dark and moody. What's the bug up your butt,?" She shuffled cards rapidly, angrily, her voice rising. "Ooh, you make me so scared." Holding the cards in one hand, she tautly bent them back, aimed them at the glowering boy, and let them fly, laughing viciously.

He swatted at the streaming cards, took a long drink, burped, pointed at her and growled. "You playin' cards or fuckin' around?"

Nina picked up the cards and reshuffled slowly, thoughtfully staring at her neighbor and schoolmate, wondering why she even bothered with this piece of crap.

"So, what's the skinny? Why the mad on all the time?"

"Who wouldn't, livin' in this nut house? Everything has to be perfect for them all the time. Mom's like a commercial from the '40's with her sickening smiles making believe all is well, just eat your supper and we will all be fine. Dad is always stompin' around like I just did somethin' wrong and he's tryin' to sniff it out, so sure he's gonna find it. Bro Eugene gets it done, makes Pops proud. I could puke. He gets the promotion at the flooring store, tells everyone how he's going to have his name next to Dad's some day, you know, Frank Guyler and Son. Sure, Eugene the son, not Greg, the screw up. And of course, there's little Samantha, the spoiled brat who gets anything she wants because she knows how to play their game. She's the master of manipulation, Nina. Always knows just when to pout and how much, then smiles and hugs her daddy and out comes the dough she wants. Me? I'm in this castle, see, with a moat all around it. Anybody comes near telling me

I ought to do this or that, or why don't I try harder, or why don't I stop doing stuff, I aim my canons at them and through the stone slits I let them have it with all my might. You got all that?"

"Sorta." She dealt out two cards to each of them. "But you're nuts and I don't care if you fire those canon, but you need to get the hell out of that fort and get your act together or you'll end up living here forever, dependent on a family that doesn't bring you joy."

"Hah." He pushed their school books roughly down the counter. "Joy? What the hell are you talking about, Nina? You talk so sissy sometime. I don't know why I put up with you." He pulled on his soda and burped. "Not me, kiddo. I'll never end up here. I would rather eat dirt by the railroad tracks. I am building up a stake playing poker here and there. I have quite a bundle already. I'm gonna be a professional poker player like those guys on TV. They don't work, they just travel around and play poker and make a fortune. And let me tell you something, they are not all that good. I know I could do way the hell better than some of those clodhoppers."

"See what I mean. You're nuts. You think you're better because you can see all the hands on TV. In person you see only your own, Ditso."

"Oh, yeah. What do you know about it?" He snorted. "You're just a stupid girl who shouldn't even be playing poker. It's for boys. I have a great hand here. You playin' or what?" He stared down at two nines.

"If you have a great hand, don't tell me, bet your cards, fool." She smiled down at two kings.

He pushed two quarters toward the center of the counter. He hunched over the two cards in his pudgy hands.

Sliding over two quarters, she turned over three cards from the deck. "Here's the flop. Ooh, a three, queen and five. Goody."

"Shut up and bet or pass. What?" His lips were tight, his eyes slitted. He ran his hand through his hair.

"You're so easy to read," she goaded. "No bet? Where's that great hand you said you had? Doesn't look so good anymore?" She turned over the street card, a three. "Oops. You have a three?"

He pushed two more quarters in. Nina did not believe him, raised it four more. Greg was forced to do the same.

"Aha. A bluffer, right? A bleedin' bluffer."

"Just show me the river, smart ass."

She turned over the last card, a five. "You betting anymore? I think you have a pair of something but I bet it's crap. The only reason you matched my bet is because of all you put in the pot. Am I right, or what?"

"What you got?" He turned over his pair of nines and looked across at her grinning face, and he felt cold at his core.

Nina giggled. "I can't help it, Guy. You're so easy." She choked laughter as she scraped in the quarters.

"Girls shouldn't play poker at all. You don't belong at a game, it's only for guys. You look goofy playing a man's game, like a lesbo or something. You just look dumb, like you're out of place."

"So do you, boy. So do you because just between you and me, you really don't know how to play. You think you do, but you have a long, long way to go to get to that television. That's just a pipe dream. You just hate it because you can't beat me because I always know what you're up to, always, because you talk and brag too much and because...."

He hurriedly pushed quarters into his hand, pocketed them along with the deck, pulled his books over to him, pushed some to her, opened binders and hissed, "A car door. The fuckin' Brady Bunch is home. Study."

They filed into the kitchen, Olivia Guyler immediately going to the fridge and removing salad makings.

Frank grabbed two beers, handed one to Eugene and said, "So we should order some of that Berber? Maybe three rolls just to try it out?"

"It's big in the southeast, I hear. And the top colors are light blue, beige and burgundy. It would be good to start with those three colors." He loosened his tie, ran his fingers through his light brown hair and tilted back to take a hit of beer.

Greg rolled his eyes at Nina. She folded up her books and rose. "That's enough studying for me for one day. See you tomorrow."

"Oh, don't go. Surely you have time for one more game. Deal me in, too." Samantha leaned her head to one side, dyed blonde hair spilling over one shoulder. She held up a king of diamonds. "Where do you suppose this came from?"

Nina blushed.

"Bug off, nosey. It's mine. I use it as a book mark." He grabbed the card out of her hand and shoved it into his history book.

"I thought you kids were studying. Cards again? Someday the cops will raid this place." Olivia rinsed her cup in the sink and placed it in the rack. She wiped her hands on a towel as she leaned her small frame against the counter. Her curly brown hair lay smooth around a thin, oval face, once pretty, now three children sad. Her first son, Eugene, was her bright light, smart, a business major now running one of their three flooring businesses. Greg was always a headache and, she knew, always would be. Samantha the baby was a willful, gorgeous, manipulative, college student who knew expertly just how to play parent against parent. It kept tensions pretty tight in the Guyler household and no matter what kind of front Olivia tried to put on, she inwardly accepted the fact that her family was not the one of her dreams.

"Hey, kid. I warned you. Not in the house. Why the hell can't you listen, you stubborn ass?" Frank banged his beer on the counter. Greg walked rapidly out of the kitchen, Nina right behind, head down. They both left the house.

"I'll walk you half way home, to Alice Street. Then I'm going to the gas station, play some real poker without any girls." He glanced at her sideways and tried to suppress a smile.

"Okay. Just don't talk about your hand. No raised eyebrows, no smiles, no bragging, no nothing, you hear me?" She held her books to her chest.

"You really think you know more about the game than I do, don't you? Well you are so wrong. When I play with the guys, I am relaxed and in total control. It's because you are a girly girl. You're hard to read because you're giddy and silly and I never can tell what you are thinking. And girls always seem to get the better hands. I notice that on TV. When the ladies get a pair, you can almost bet that one of the flop cards will give her trips. You ever watch?" As they walked along the sidewalk, he tended to drift to his right, giving her a little bump.

"You off balance or something, Guyler?" She bopped him in the shoulder with her little fist. "I don't like to watch poker on TV. It's boring. But when I play it's not. Sometimes the chess club ends up in a poker game when we practice at each other's houses. Then it's fun, way more challenging than chess. It's just guys and gals in any order, not like you think it should be girls against the guys or some silly shit like that. You are so queer. And I never noticed any sex getting any better deals. It's all the same to me. I told you you're batty. You see everything the way you walk....off balance and some day it will get you in trouble, you'll see."

"I can't talk to you. You think you know everything. Here's where I turn. See you around, Miss Genius."

"You need to finish the math, remember?"

"Jesus, even my mother doesn't give a shit if I finish the math. Why do you care?"

"So you don't flunk, have to repeat the year which means another year to put up with your bullshit."

"You are one strange broad. If you're so worried, do the math for me."

"Do your own damn math. I do enough for you as it is. Try to use math in your poker playing. You might actually win a game or two."

He put up his hand as a wave of dismissal.

She watched Greg Guyler saunter along the sidewalk, his gait a little awkward, his head tilted to the left a bit, sort of like the leaning tower of Pisa. If only he weren't such a pain in the neck he'd be a half-decent study partner and close friend. She smiled, shook her head and turned down her street to home.

Chapter 7

"Cripes, Guyler. You bettin' or diggin' your nose, or what?" Charlie, 'Stretch' Ritchie leaned back on his chair holding his cards against his chest. Wrapping his long legs around the front of the rungs, he tilted dangerously back, glaring across the table at a frowning Greg. "C'mon, already. Do something. I have work tomorrow and it's getting late."

"All right. You probly got me beat, but I have to bet my cards. I know, I know. Okay, I'm gonna see your forty and raise ya eighty more." He flipped the chips into the middle of the table and stared with hooded eyes at Stretch.

Through the open, high, barred window of the back room of the gas station, the soft sound of the dings of gas being delivered to someone's tank was the only sound as the boys stared at the pot, their cards and each other.

"Let's have a flop there, Jimmy." The dealer turned over two jacks and a ten of diamonds.

Stretch bent his head down to his two cards and contemplated his king of clubs and queen of spades.

"Two hundred," he said softly.

"Shit. What do you have, two pair?" He folded his arms across his chest and blew air out of his puffed cheeks. He reached down and peeked at his jack of diamonds and eight of spades. "I'll see your two hundred."

The boys at the table watched the flop, the two players and the large pot.

The turn card was a five of hearts. Both players checked, waiting for the river card. Jimmy slowly turned the card over, revealing a nine of clubs. Stretch had a straight, beating Greg's three jacks.

"God damn you, Stretch. You just about cleaned me out. Jesus, I hate those cards….they always go against me at the wrong time."

"That's it. I gotta go."

Greg pulled the cards to his beefy hands and began to shuffle.

"C'mon, one more hand. I still have some dough. Who's in?"

The pretzels were almost gone, Greg's beer was flat and he just didn't know what to do. He had been looking at his hand for over ten minutes and the natives were getting restless.

"Let's go, Guyler. Shit or get off the pot." Eddie twisted two poker chips through his fingers. He glared.

"All right. Hold your water, Edward." Greg glanced over at his schoolmate since the fourth grade. They were never really close, but always orbiting each other in their Westchester neighborhood. "Whatta you got? Two pair? Or the flush?" He looked down at the flop and the street card, two jacks, hearts and clubs, a six and a ten of clubs. In his tight-fisted hand he held a ten of hearts and an ace of diamonds.

"I'm all in, bonehead. You ain't got nothing." Greg pushed his chips to the center of the table and snapped over his cards.

Eddie smiled at the two pair and tossed his cards face up to the center next to Greg's two cards. He had a seven of clubs and a queen of hearts.

Greg stood up. "C'mon, c'mon, no clubs. Please no clubs. I need a break here."

The dealer slowly turned over the river card, an ace of diamonds. Greg blew out air in relief and punched his fist over his head. "Yes. For once, a winner."

"Goddamit, you never bet your cards right. I'm never playing with you again, asswipe."

"Is that a promise, Prince Edward? Okay when old Greg loses, but look out when he wins once in a while. Well, I know how to win, too, buddy." He scooped in his winnings. It was a rare moment and he wanted to savor it, wanted it to last.

"Let me tell you something, Eddie. That felt so good I'll be dreaming about it tonight, that ace of diamonds flippin' over in slow motion, making me beat your ass. It's the sweetest thing on Earth and I love it. See you guys next time."

One by one the boys rose, swung jackets around, shrugged into them and began to leave with grunts of tomorrow's obligations. Greg, too, placed the cards in the middle of the table, turned off the overhead light and passed through the station out into the cool night.

"All right. See you tomorrow. Same time, same station, morons."

They drifted off in different directions muttering their okays and good nights.

Greg slung his jacket over his shoulder and left. On the way home, he walked fast, thoughts of perfect poker flops burning his psyche. He had to prove he could do it consistently, be a winner. He'd show Eddie and the rest of that freak table that he could do it, could come out on top. But most of all, he wanted to tell Krepelli that she is so wrong about his style of play. He'd show her, too, her and that big yapper of hers, always ragging on him, making him feel like he didn't know what he was doing. He'd show them all.

Chapter 8

The refrigerator door was open. Greg lay the bottles of beer flat on the bottom shelf. He slammed the door shut, put the snacks in the pantry and started for the stairs. He heard the front door open and the high-pitched voices of his niece, Emma and his nephew, Stevie.

"Damn," he muttered. "Samantha." Before he made it to the steps, the four and five year olds were tugging at his shirt tail.

"Unca Geggy. We want ice cream." He lifted them both up to his chest and whispered in their ears, "Ask your mommy."

She shot him a grim look. "Can't you interact with your family? Where's Dad? Why aren't you at the store?"

He set the children down. They ran from the room to the kitchen.

"Didn't feel like going in today. Since he started that little furniture line, guess who moves the shit around? He doesn't care. They're doing that inventory stuff anyway. It's boring. You should go down and help out, make a few bucks legitimately. You know, like a part time job. Instead of coming here for checks all the time. Know what I mean?"

She sat on the sofa and tucked her long, tan legs under her. He stared at her for a minute. He took a long pull on his beer.

"Why are you wasting yourself? You should be married, give the kids a daddy figure, go back to school and you know, be normal instead of making babies you can't raise." He flopped down on the bottom step of the stairs, his arms on his knees.

"Hey, knucklehead, at least I'm on mother's assistance, in my own apartment and, I think I'm raising my kids pretty well all by my lonesome. If I got married, believe me, it would be like having a third child under foot. God, I miss Mom. She was such a big help to me. But, I have plans, don't worry about me. And look who's talking. Of the three of us, you're the biggest leech. What the hell do you do most of your time anyway? At least when Mom was alive she made you pitch in and help out a little. She tried to put on the front, like you'll be okay, you just need to find out what you really want. So what do you do? You play poker. Shit, you're not even good at it. I beat you all the time, Nina Krepelli beats you forever, even Eddie stays ahead of you." She tapped her head. "And Eddie's a little, you know, slow. Is there anyone in this whole town that you can beat?"

"Is that right? I hold my own around here, enough to have money in my pocket for the things I need. I'm doin' all right for your information. And if it wasn't for me, that store would always look seedy. I'm the one keeps it clean, moves the crap around until it looks good and goes out on the flooring jobs more than anyone else. But is that good enough? Hell no. It's Eugene the Giant gets all the pats on the back for the Joe college marketing ideas. Big pump. And, Missy, I am going to a tournament in Tunica, Mississippi next week. I'm all set to come home with quite a bank roll. You'll see, smarty, you'll see."

"Yeah? Does Dad know you'll be out of the store next week? They get busy after inventory with the sales and all. But I bet you go even if he gets pissed off. You're so into yourself. Like no one else counts, or something. Then you lose, you'll come home with your tail between your legs, you'll see. You should take one of those poker buddies with you to keep you out of trouble. Because, Bro, if there is trouble, it will find you. Remember where you heard it."

"The store will be fine without me. I won't even be missed. After all, Prince Eugene will be there sucking up to Dad, taking over the way he always does. Lately he even brings his Shelley in to help out. Not that she's much help, does more shopping than pitching in. Last time she was in she took home two lamps, a runner, two glass-topped end tables and a wine rack."

"Sweet. But I can't complain. Dad furnished my apartment for me. He's good that way."

"What way? I wonder what I'd get if I had my own apartment. Hell, I'd have to work my ass off to get stuff."

"That's how it's usually done, Shylock."

"Except for Shelley and little Samantha. Hey, here's an idea for you. Why don't you go after those two deadbeat dads? Some child support would help you out a lot, wouldn't it?"

She waved her hand parallel to the floor. "Ixnay. And I'd appreciate it if you didn't talk about that with Dad. It's a sensitive subject. I want nothing to do with that part of my life. That's past and the less said, the better. And my kids don't ever have to know about daddies. I am going to be enough."

His smile was crooked. "No worries there, Missy. The last thing Dad and I do is talk, I mean about anything. Usually, he barks because of something I did or he thought I did. You know how it is."

*****

Most men Frank Guyler's age were getting a middle-aged spread, losing hair and generally beginning to look long in the tooth. Not Frank. He was a vigorous sixty-three year old with a head of thick, dark curly hair softly sprayed with grey, a flat stomach with a narrow waist and straight white teeth. He didn't smile much but when he did, usually at his two grandchildren, his eyes shined with the intensity of silver. Although not a tall man, his energetic movements made him look in command and control.

"The sale is in two days. Make sure that a lot of the smaller stuff is up front, like lamps, footstools, some of that metal furniture, like last year. We did real good with those items. Eugene had the right idea. Put the pick quick stuff where people have to trip over them on their way out of the store. You know, like, hey, I should get one of those. See?"

He nodded. "I'll get it done before ten, just like always. Where is the idea man anyway? I could use some help movin' this shit around. Never mind. Those thinking types just get in my way. Couple of the guys are gonna stop in to help out and play some poker. I need to practice. There's this tournament in Tunica starting next weekend. After the entrance fee and the room bill, it's still under a grand. You don't need me that week. Eugene will be there to run the place. Five days or so isn't all that long. What do you say?"

Frank hunched up his shoulders. "Your mother's passing was a blessing is what I say. I just don't care. Don't call me for anything because I will be busy. Your timing is lousy, real lousy. We're coming into a busy season. The furniture items are new territory for me. Before you go I expect you to do that re-arranging we do for the impulse buying, he calls it. I'll throw in two hundred but that's all. You need to earn the rest. Okay? I don't think you play good poker. You can beat some of those punks you play with but mostly they're brain dead. A tournament in Tunica will have real live wires. You'll never last. But, go on, make an ass of yourself."

"Yeah. I appreciate your concern."

"Don't be a wise ass. If it wasn't for me there wouldn't be any poker. Remember, just don't call me when you get in trouble like you always do. I mean it. I'm way too busy for you. You hear? And keep this place clean. I don't want to have to clean up after you bums. Be sure they don't flop all over the furniture. Back room only. There's a storm warning out for tonight anyway, so get your asses home early."

"Be out of here before midnight. The guys have work tomorrow so we'll break up after a few hands."

"Well, at least some people have a sense of responsibility. Where the hell could you work where you'd go in every other day whether you like it or not? Eh? Where could you get a job?"

Not wanting another argument, Greg went to the side wall of the showroom and carefully lifted a small lacy metal table, carried it to the front window and set it next to a glider rocker. As his father walked down the aisle to the front door, Greg glanced sideways at him.

"I will also get that flooring laid in Queens. That's a big job. It's a job Eugene the thinker couldn't do in a hundred years. But old Greg will get it done and it will look good, too."

"Yeah, yeah. Whatever. Just keep this place clean like I said."

He watched his father back out of the reserved space, and turn right out of the parking lot. Greg watched the taillights disappear into traffic and wondered where the old man was heading. Home was to the left. He pushed a table into place, shrugged and tossed a pillow into the corner of a sofa. Turning quickly, he walked down the aisle between overstuffed chairs, sofas and racks of flooring samples to the back office. Twenty minutes later, Eddie, Greco and Tiny came through the front door, threw the latch and headed down the aisle.

"If I get wiped out, this red leather sofa is mine." Eddie flopped his square frame into the soft, shiny back, his head against the puffy upholstery. He ran his hand through his thick black hair and laughed.

"C'mon, you playing cards or what?" Greco was built like a young janitor, squat, pear-shaped, his brown hair clipped. He had short arms and the beginning of a gut that would be forever hard to lose. He stood in the middle of the aisle shaking out of his black leather jacket.

Tiny was really a small fellow. His thin red hair framed a narrow, freckled face sharply divided by a long, pointed nose. A too skinny neck disappeared between two sharp bony shoulders. He looked around the showroom, hands deep in his jeans pockets.

"Yo, Guyler. We're here. Where the hell are you?" Tiny's voice was a pitch too high to be masculine. He bounced up and down on his toes, the others chuckled.

He came out of the back office. "I'm here. I was in the can. Did you do-do birds bring any money? Let's go. The old man said a storm's comin' in. He's real worried about me"

"Yeah, right. Like my old man would be worried about me. He just doesn't want us to mess anything up around here, right?" Eddie pulled a cigarette out of his shirt pocket and started to light up.

"That's it, genius. You are so smart it scares me. No smoking out here. Come on in the office. There's ash trays. You know the drill. Don't give me any problems. I got enough of my own."

Three hands later, Greg held the deck, fluttered the edges a few times as he stared at the trio.

"What?" Tiny's light red eyebrows arched up inquisitively. "You got something on your mind or what?"

"Can you tell if I'm bluffin? I told you about the tournament and I was just wondering, you know, if I give anything away?"

Greco snorted. "Here we go. It's tournament time and the big shot wants some tips from the experts."

"What's wrong with that? Can't you help a buddy out? No shit. I know you can tell if I have a crap hand, but how? You remember Nina? Nina Krepelli from over on Alice Street? She could always tell what I was holdin' but she never would tell me how she knew."

The three looked at each other and started to laugh, Tiny almost choking on his beer.

"Maybe she didn't want you just holding cards, dumb ass. Did you ever think of that?" Eddie asked through a wide grin.

"Who? Nina? And me? Get the hell out of here. She was always more boy than girl. That's why I didn't mind playing poker with her. Hell, I could never play with a real girl."

More side glances and lewd laughter. Greco punched the table. "Jesus, Guyler. Do you hear yourself? You don't like to play with girls. You nuts or something?"

"You know what I mean. Girls do not belong at a poker table. It's a man's game, like football, professional baseball and sports like that. Look, if you play against them and beat them, everyone says what a sissy, he beat a girl, big deal. And if you lose to them, it's even worse, like, wow, you got beaten by a girl, aren't you ashamed. You're damned if you do and damned if you don't. See?"

Tiny crushed out his smoke. "Yeah. I can see that. I played in Little League once when there was a girl on the other team. It didn't feel right. They should have their own leagues, like the softball, they're great at softball."

Eddie frowned as he put a pretzel in his mouth. "Usually, I can't tell if someone is bluffing because, see, I'm a real poker player. I play my own cards. I don't give a shit what you have. If my pair looks good to me, I put my dough out there. You think too much. All this manure about trying to figure out what the other guy has is overrated, far as I'm concerned. Oh, don't get me wrong, there are times when the betting gets out of hand and I need to wonder which way the wind is blowing, but mostly I stand by my hand." He flicked salt off his chest.

"So you're telling me you never bluff. Never? You're so full of it, Eddie. C'mon, how can you tell if I have a good hand or a crap hand?"

Eddie sighed. "Because you're easy, is what. If you got a good hand, those lips of yours go tight and white like you just saw a rattler, or something. If you're bluffin' you keep lookin' at us to see if we know. You're like a little kid who doesn't know how to lie yet."

"Can we just play some poker now?" Tiny whined. "It's getting late and that thunder out there doesn't sound good. I have to go all the way to Queens tonight, to my sister."

"The hell with it. You guys are no help anyway. Put your garbage in that can and get going. I need to straighten up. I don't know why I ever thought you jokers could help. I don't need any help, hell, I know what I'm doing, you'll see." He put the cards in a file cabinet drawer.

Eddie slapped Greg on the shoulder. "They're going to eat you alive, you know. You won't know what hit you. Probably be finished the first day. Forget about finishing in the money, honey. No way."

"I'll remember those words of wisdom, Pal. Then I'll make you eat them. You'll see. All of you. You'll see."

"Hey, Guyler," Greco shouted from the aisle. "This is like the couch and recliner my folks just bought. Good stuff. And my old man said he got the best deal right here from your old man."

"Once in a while I can bring in a customer or two. Guess the old boy knows how to treat people, most people, anyway. All right, Ratsos, see you around. Thanks for all those neat tips. I'm going to do just fine. Now get goin' bums, so I can lock up."

Chapter 9

"It's nice to see you, Greg. How have you been, anyhow? Still living in Westchester with, you know?" Nina tried not to smile. The years were kind to her. Thirty five and she looked about twenty six. She had filled in all the right places, stayed thin, chic, sported short cropped blonde tufted hair. Her wide smile, though, was still as honest and sincere as it was when she was in high school.

He, on the other hand, put on about thirty pounds, was pear-shaped with a thick chin and a receding hairline, but his hair was still black and curly. Nina thought his eyes still held promise, that the real Greg was inside, somewhere.

Hey, Nina. Long time. Look at you. You are a sight to these tired eyes. What brings you to Westchester? Slumming?" He stood in the aisle pushing a cart half full of bottles of soda, two loaves of bread, can of coffee, and a large bag of chips. She held a jug of chocolate milk at her side.

"I see you still like to snack. Big game at your pad tonight?"

"Nah. I'm still at the old homestead. You were right. You always said I'd end up there. After my mother passed away, I couldn't leave the old man alone. You know how it is."

"What a crock. You couldn't stand your father and I bet you still can't. As I remember, it was a fight a day with you two." She hefted her jug onto the edge of his cart.

"Yeah, well, it's not too bad. He lets me help out at the Westchester store. It's the biggest one. Eugene manages the other one, the one in Rye. He doesn't come around too much. And Samantha, she's been through two hubbies, knows how to find the losers. She only comes around when she needs money. The family is basically rotted out. He leaned heavily on the cart handle. "So, you still teaching in Nyack?"

"And loving it. The school by the Hudson. What a view. The pay is good, the kids are motivated, great parents, nice condo by the bridge and summers off." She flashed a him a bright smile. "You'll have to visit sometime. We could play poker on the screened deck, watch the boats go up and down the river."

He rolled his eyes. "I'd beat you silly. I'm a pretty good player now. I've been in a few tourneys and I have regular games in the city, too. I win enough to keep me goin'. You seeing someone?"

"Not in my circle. The men teachers are too up tight, full of themselves, always competing for the principal's pat on the ass."

"He pat your ass once in a while?"

"He's a grandpa. So you still show your hand, right? I'd put money on it. After all this time you should play like a pro. Sure, enough to get by," she scoffed.

"Nice seein' you, hot shot teacher. I see you're still alone, so don't make any fun of my poker play. Only reason you beat me so much is 'cause you're a girl. Shouldn't be playin' poker anyway. It's a man's game and always will be." He started to push his cart down the aisle. She kept up with him.

"If you could beat me, you wouldn't care if I was a gorilla. But you can't, so you take it out on all the ladies. You're so transparent when it comes to poker. I don't know how you ever win any hands at all. If you still make your face into a circus before you lay a bet, you better keep that job at your family flooring business." She poked him in the arm.

Greg suppressed a smile. "So you're not seeing anyone?"

"I'm waiting for you, Guyler. See, you never could read me, loser. Didn't even ask me to the prom after all those poker lessons I gave you."

"Hah. You never showed me anything. Always so secretive. You never let me see if you were bluffing or not. Some lessons, you always giggling every time I folded." He turned the cart toward the checkout stations.

"Hey, dummy. That was the lesson, the not knowing. It's all a mystery, a mind game. You must be playing with guys like you." She glanced at him sideways. "I'm right, right?"

"Is that right? For your information, I'm going to be in a big tournament in Tunica next month. I'll show you what I can do, sister. I'll shut your big mouth up real fast."

Nina shifted the milk to her other hand. "Bet you don't even finish in the money. Not that I don't have a little faith in you, but those real players will eat you alive. You don't have the finesse to control a table. Let me know how you make out, okay?"

"I will. Heck, this isn't my first tournament, or anything. I'm a regular in these tournaments now. What do you want to bet I finish in the top five?" He started to place his purchases on the counter.

"Hmm. How about a real date, flowers, wine, dinner, the works. And you being real nice, you know, normal. See if you could pull that off." Her temples turned a soft shade of pink.

"Me and you? There's a bet. What's wrong with ten dollars, or maybe even a twenty?" He continued to lay out his order, carefully pulled two coupons out of his wallet and placed one on the chips and the other on the sour cream. He told the cashier that they were the correct brands.

Nina shook her head. "Okay, a twenty it is. That will be the easiest twenty I'll ever make."

He waited while she checked out and they left the store. She bumped his side. "Hey, maybe I should go with you, you know, keep you out of trouble, coach you on how to play the game correctly." She put her hand on a lean hip, pushed a stray strand of curly hair behind her ear. "What do you think?"

He slammed the back door. "What kind of trouble? It's only a poker tournament, for God's sake. I been in plenty of them. And I don't need any coachin' from a girl. Besides, now you want to coach after all those years of scooping in pots without telling me what you had. I don't need that kind of stress. Just spend your summer pestering your family."

"Do me a favor, Guyler. Watch how you dress in case they videotape the tourney."

"Why? Now what? Are you suddenly the fashion police? Jeez, it's always something with you."

Tossing her hair off her shoulder, she stared at him and decided to let go of something that bothered her for years.

"See, you're the type of guy that, no matter how fancy schmancy he tries to dress, there's always that little twist that's, you know, like out of place. When you showed up at the prom, for instance, you wore that powder blue tux with the burgundy shirt and white tie. You greased your hair back and you smelled like a gallon of Aqua-Velva. Remember? But I felt that if I looked closely enough, real close, you know, I'd find the tiniest bit of shit somewhere. Could be at the hem of your pants, the side of your shoe, but I knew, in my heart of hearts that it was there." She headed for her car.

"You're so full of it," he said to her back. "Just get that twenty ready. I'll call you when I get back so we can arrange to meet so I can collect my winnings from you, Miss know-it-all."

He put sunglasses on as he eased into the front seat of the car, ran his fingers through his gelled black hair, revved the engine, and started to back out of the parking slot. She leaned into the window, her face close, a tress of hair falling over her shoulder.

"So you're not going to tell me what happened? Just going to drive off and leave me here wondering? I thought we were pretty good friends, good enough to tell each other things, you know, like we used to."

He exhaled, eyes straight ahead. "You're the same pain in the ass you always been, Nina, and I guess you'll never change."

"I know. So what was it, assault, rape, consensual sex gone bad, were you drunk, or what? I remember that girl. A pesky, nosey busy body. She get under your skin finally? My aunt told me your lawyer got you off, then she dropped the charges. Fill me in."

"I'll make it short or your milk is gonna go sour. It wasn't me. Remember Philip, the kid with the bad acne? He had a spring break party at the family cottage at the Jersey shore. We were all juniors, Tiny and I at the tech school, the others at colleges around here and there. Philip invited everyone he could think of. I went down on the last day, Sunday. By six I was pretty buzzed. I only remember Mona came by me, took my arm and led me outside to the beach. Next thing I know, there's a bunch of guys and girls around us, some shovin' back and forth, her screamin' her ass off, then here come the cops to break it all up, shoving everyone back. Then I realized I was on the ground in the center of everyone. After all the dust settled, she accused me of all the usual crap but Philip admitted that he got pissed off at me because I went outside with 'his' girl, laying on the beach. She was just trying to get his goat because they had a fight. He roughed her up quite a bit but then he blamed it on me, that I instigated it, you know, to save his face. I guess she did it to make him jealous or something. They are one queer couple. At the hearing a lot of their so-called friends told weird tales about those two. So there, anything else? Oh, yeah. After the case was over, I caught up with that weasel and almost pulled his ears off. I told him to marry Mona as soon as possible before she finds a freak richer than he is."

Nina stood, hands on the door frame. "You'll never change, Guyler. Always settling things your way. Hey, bet your Daddy really dug all that action, eh?"

"Move away from the car. I gotta go." He watched Nina walk slowly to her parking spot, caught in his rearview mirror. He leaned over as he glided along, keeping her in his sight. He continued watching her until she reached her car.

"Still gets under my skin, that royal pain in the ass. Wish I could beat the little bitch, just once." He sat and thought about the long, cool period of time in the Guyler household when his father wouldn't even look at Greg, like he was a piece of dirt, even though the lawyer got him off and those two pismires dropped the charges. Frank Guyler still acted like his son was as guilty as a confessed serial killer. He sighed.

Driving out of the parking lot, she turned up the music. "Schmuck loser. A poker tournament yet, yeah, sure. He won't even make a money table. I only hope there are about a half dozen girls there who beat his ass good." She turned onto the highway that led to her aunt's house. She giggled to herself. "At least six girls who will be able to beat the crap out of that egotistical little rat."

Chapter 10

"Mr. Olsen, are you feeling all right? Sit down for a while." Kat Pearse led the red-faced, stocky gentleman to a bench seat against the wall near a wide window overlooking Liberty Avenue in South Knoxville.. It was Mr. Olsen's third dance lesson at Kat's Sunlight Dance Studio. Traffic moved smoothly outside under a grey, threatening sky. He leaned back against the cushioned seat and closed his eyes.

"Take a breather. You've been working hard at this waltz. You're doing beautifully, I might add." She smiled as he puffed out his cheeks, exhaling loudly.

"I'm okay. I just never thought that this would be so damn hard. You're a great teacher, Kat. Who would ever think that a tank like me could float across a dance floor and look half decent? How is Jen doing?"

Kat put her small hand over his warm, pudgy fingers. "Jon tells me she's a whiz, picks up the steps quickly and is as smooth as silk."

"I knew it. My Jen has always been good at everything. We want to do our daughter proud at this wedding. We need to show our circle at the country club that we love our daughter so much we took dance lessons to honor her when it's time to get up to dance. She chose that slow song, 'The First Time Ever I Saw Your Face' as the first dance. Jen and I want to do the song some justice. But we might just die trying, right?" Steve Olsen leaned heavily against the seat.

"You'll both do fine. Next time you come in, you'll begin dancing together. Jonathon and I feel you're both ready now. But let's not overdo it. One more time around the floor?"

"Sure. Easy for you to say, young lady. You're the one with all these trophies decorating the studio. What are they for, anyway?"

She held out her arms and they began to smoothly maneuver the polished dance floor.

"They're mostly from dance competitions around the country. Some of them belong to Jon, too. He danced with me on Broadway for a while, then tried a few ballet productions. He's very versatile and a very good teacher."

"So are you."

Mr. and Mrs. Olsen were on lesson three of a ten lesson series, twice a week, an hour each session, fifteen dollars each. Sixty dollars a week for each couple, usually a half dozen couples, plus a handful of teens polishing their skills, some choreography for local groups and instructions at the schools for musicals kept the Sunlight Studio fairly lucrative.

Kat's dad, Ron Pearse, worked on construction projects in the booming Knoxville area. After Kat's many successes, the logical step was to open a dance studio of her own. Ron pitched in and, with the help of his contacts, had the professional studio up and ready in a short time. Kat loved it the moment she set foot inside.

Mr. Olsen rose from the bench, stretched his arms above his head and sighed. "Enough rest. I have to get to the tailor for a tux fitting and that sky does not look good."

"A wedding at the country club must be fabulous. I've seen pictures in the Sunday Life section but I've never been there. It must be impressive. She took his arm and walked him to the door.

"It is unique. Say, why don't you and Jonathon have dinner with me and the Mrs. this Sunday? Members need to clock some spending hours once in a while to stay on the active list. We have to keep the place going, you know."

"You're required to log in hours at the dining room?" Kat was amazed.

Olsen glided around a corner. "The pro shop, the gift shop, special events, charity tournaments, and so on. I love to play golf and I enjoy all the amenities so I don't mind going along with their programs. This Sunday then, all right? Come about seven. We'll show you around before dinner."

The music came to a soft string and wind end as Olsen gently bent his knees in a dip and gracefully bowed to her.

"Very well done. You did the corner perfectly and the shoulders were up where they're supposed to be. You feeling okay now?"

He hugged her. "I feel fine. I'm putting a lot of work into this one dance and at my age, I get a little pooped after an hour of dancing with a dynamo like you. I didn't realize how out of shape I was until I agreed to take these lessons. Believe me, no more golf cart."

She pulled at both ends of a fluffy towel around her neck, blonde pony tail across her left shoulder.

"You'll end up in such great shape I bet your game improves and you'll put time in at those country club dances. You and the Mrs. should try some Latin dance lessons next."

"There you go." He pointed at her. "See you and Jonathon around seven then."

She watched him from the window as he eased into his Lincoln Town Car. Thinking back to her own wedding, she shook her head at the contrast as she recalled her mom's words.

"No, honey, you can't have a white gown and an aisle if you're five months pregnant. Ted Sims can ask his parents to come here for dinner after the civil ceremony. We'll get you a bouquet and an outfit from Gardner's. Get Susan to be witness for you, and he can ask his brother. Other than that, what else?"

Ginny Pearse had accepted her daughter's common, but none-the-less upsetting dilemma by constantly trying to find a bright spot.

"Maybe we can all get along, you know, for the sake of the baby. We can spend holidays together, the two families. They seem like nice people. I can baby sit and you can continue at dance school, still be in the competitions, and be a happy family, the three of you." Her shoulders shook as her litany came to an end, punctuated by a sob.

Although Ted Sims was only twenty when he fell in love with the nineteen year old dancer, he was not an unfocussed young man. He had been working along with his father and older brother at Sims' Lake Forest Motors since he was a high school sophomore. Now, at twenty, he had his own apartment, a small car, and was working on a business degree. He explained to Kat that he'd marry her for the sake of the baby.

"You know, to give it a name and all. It's the honorable thing to do. But, I do plan to get my MBA and hopefully take over the business from my dad one day."

"Yes, Ted. It's the honorable thing to do. And the rest of it, the us in all this?" She stared at his face. Ted Sims was the most honest man she knew. Kat loved every facet of his handsome demeanor, his blue-grey eyes, short clipped dark brown hair, even the little tic in the corner of his mouth, the tic that told her more than Ted was saying. A tiny gesture that told her the truth, that he no longer loved her feverishly, but felt an obligation, a duty that was honor bound to keep. He'd be a fair husband and a dutiful father, but his priorities would be elsewhere.

At that point, she decided to call his offer and go all in. After all, the baby would have his father's name and receive his due from the well-to-do auto people. Tyler Sims was shared by four doting grandparents and a father who taught him the importance of education, business and money. Tyler soaked it all up like a sponge, wheeling and dealing at Sims' Lake Forest Motors from when he was in high school, learning the varied levels of running a business and enjoying it all, through college and graduate school. Kat smiled to herself. After the divorce, she and Ted remained on friendly terms, shared custody, worked out the holiday visits and even bought each other thoughtful gifts in Tyler's name.

"Here sport. Give this necklace to Mom. Sign your name here on the card." Ted held Tyler's hand and guided the little fingers as together they spelled 'Mom' a bit crooked, lovingly shaky.

And as the years went by, with alimony and the help of her construction Dad, Kat established her fine dancing studio with a loyal clientele who spread the word about the benefits of the Sunlight Dance workouts. People like the Olsens became a staple for her along with the diet and exercise crowd. As word spread, her business boomed.

After Mr. Olsen left the studio, Kat showered, dressed and went to her office to do some paper work. The dance team from the high school took over the studio for a one-hour rehearsal. They often rented the studio to keep their moves under wraps until the actual event.

"Hey, Kat." Jonathon sat in a leather, winged-back chair, long legs stretched out on the plush red carpet.

"Hey, yourself. How's it going with Jen Olsen? Can we start them together at the next lesson?"

Jonathon Parks was her assistant and pretty much ran the business smoothly. He'd rather dance than date, plus he had a solid sense of advertising practices, kept the ads up to date, ran the pro shop and whatever else needed attention. The two other instructors, Annie and Marty were part-timers, gym teachers at the local high school who generated classes for prom-going teens.

"Sure. The Olsens. Yes, we can schedule them for five lessons before the wedding. I watched him dance with you. Take it easy on the old boy, Kat. Sometimes we don't realize the strain involved on their creaky bods. He looked a tad peaked during his last time on the floor."

"I know." She pushed papers to the side of the desk. "He just wants to make his daughter proud on her wedding day. He's trying pretty hard but he'll be just fine. He is very light on his feet for a heavy man. By the way, he invited me to the country club to see the set-up for the wedding. Want to go with me? Maybe we can have them twirl around after dinner, you know, check out the entrance, the floor, and so on."

"Sure. Dinner at the country club, eh? We are moving on up, sweetie. Let's see if we can have them dance in the doorway first, then glide onto the floor like we did with that last event, the retirement dinner." His eyes were bright. Jonathon was planning the entrance, the dance, even the finish where they traded partners with the bride and the groom. "Is it okay with them if I go?"

She didn't tell him that Olsen had invited Jon, too. She wanted him to feel that it was sort of like a date.

"You'll be my guest, silly. We are their instructors, after all. Isn't it natural for us to be together with them on a professional basis?" Her voice shook at the end. He frowned at her questioningly.

She hesitated a moment, then sat heavily in her soft desk chair. "Damn it, Jon. Am I ever going to get over Ted Sims? Why do I always feel guilty after all these years. My God, here I am wallowing around in my forties and still emotionally tied to the man. What does it take to cut that cord?"

He rose and walked around the desk, took her hand in his and pulled her up to him. Leading her to the door, he flipped the stereo system on and selected soft rock.

"Dance with me."

They glided expertly around the polished floor to the gentle music. He guided her, their arms extended, feet sure, in control, one with the music that filled their souls. Swaying before a twirl, he whispered softly in her ear, "You may have missed a few wedding dances, but you're fulfilled every time you perform like this. Every day can be your wedding day."

The music ended smoothly as he arched her backward and held the pose. He looked down into her face, his voice suddenly loud and strident.

"Or marry me, do the wedding dances and finally be done with the Goddamned thing."

Her eyes went wide, her lips taut. Then she let go ending in a heap on the floor. Sitting next to her, he began to laugh. Kat joined in, giggling uncontrollably.

"You are insane, you know." She coughed through spasms of laughter.

He shrugged. "It's a sensible insanity if you'd just think about it."

She stood and grabbed his hand, pulling him to his feet. "We need to re-focus and get ready for the four-o'clocks. That group of eight from the high school, remember? We need to get them started for about half an hour until Annie and Marty get here from the gym. Chop, chop, Sweetie."

"Yes, Ma'am. Sure thing. Sweetie, my foot. Hey, Kat, how old is your boy, now? About 23 or 24? That's a lot of years to be indebted to the perfect daddy. Way too many years. And what about you? Are you going live in admiration of Sims forever? He's good, I admit, but you're a good mom, too.
Why feel some sort of sick guilt about the whole thing? I'm no psychologist, but, you know, isn't it supposed to end sometime?"

As she left the studio, she pulled the door shut with a loud snap.

****

Jen Olsen was animated, smoothing the tablecloth and handling the silverware as she spoke. The dining room at the country club was tastefully decorated with powder blue table linen, an abundance of crystal, and flowers in every corner. In one corner, a pianist provided soft background music against a backdrop of oversized windows, sparkling chandeliers, and well-dressed diners.

"I've ordered dusty rose tablecloths and napkins. That color will look nice with this light oak paneling, don't you think? Oh, and the centerpieces will be Asiatic lilies with babies' breath." She put her hand on Jonathon's arm, her eyes wide.

"It sounds just perfect. You folks are putting a lot of effort into this party, so it can't go wrong. What about it, Kat?" He stirred his coffee by hitting the bottom of the cup a few times. Kat cringed. Inside, she managed a tiny smile, though.

"Well, Jon, it's more than a party. It's an event and one that will make the Sunday Lifestyles section. More than that, though, you are both creating an experience, a memory, that will last in your family for a long time. I think it's great that you're so involved. Not too many parents go this overboard."

Mrs. Olsen smiled at her. "In our circle they do. Not that we're trying to outdo anyone, or something like that. But since we have all this available to us, and we love our daughter and her fiancé so very much, well, why not?"

"I agree. Mrs. Olsen, will that arched entrance be decorated, you know, with flowers or drapery?"

"Please, call me Jen. Jon does. I guess because we dance so closely." She leaned into her husband's shoulder. "We are Jen and Steve, dear. Yes, the arch will be lined with gardenias. Steve, what did that director say about the entrance?"

"After Patti and Michael have their first dance, then you and I enter under the arch, dance half a song, then you switch to Michael and I twirl around with Patti until almost the end, then we switch back. And I'm really nervous about it all."

"Don't be," Kat said. "It sounds pretty easy and we'll keep at those steps until they are second nature to you both. If you stand under the arch for a few seconds and start to dance from there onto the dance floor, I think you'll make a more dramatic entrance rather than just walking out, stopping and then starting to dance."

"I like it." Jen clasped her hands together. "Picture it, Steve. Patti will be so proud. You two have such good ideas. I suppose it comes from working together on creative projects."

Kat was aware of voices rising over the soft dinner music. She tried to determine the location and finally pinpointed a loud outburst coming from behind a closed door near the double doors that led to the kitchen.

Steve smiled as Kat squinted questioningly at him. "So what's behind door number three? It sounds familiar but out of place here." She gestured at the dining room with her outstretched arm.

"You are so right." Jen's tone was close to a hiss. "And I told the manager that the wedding day would be off limits to their shenanigans."

"Since part of their ante goes to the country club, the board decided that two days a week would be fine for poker evenings and that it would count toward their time commitment for social events here at the club. It's harmless. Doc Parker, Jack Brown from the school board, Amy Grand, the fire chief's secretary and so on, all participate. Mostly they do it for fun but they do get loud. Let's finish up here and I'll take you into the inner sanctum."

"That does not make it right. Poker in a back room just sounds sleazy to me, Steve. I know you approve but if I ever get on the board, well, just look out." Jen set her coffee cup onto the saucer noisily.

Jonathon leaned toward her. "May I have a ride home with you? Kat drove and I don't feel like waiting around while she indulges in that so-called friendly game."

She stared at Kat. "I'm surprised. You play poker? Wherever did you pick up that vice?"

Kat laughed. "My dad worked construction and his crowd was a beer and poker night group. He taught me the finer points of the game when I was around five or so. He kept telling me how good I was at it until I finally believed him. Then I tested myself at a few back room games with friends, then a few tournaments, and today, I can hold my own against the best of them."

Jon rolled his eyes at Jen. "She can, too. She plays as well as she dances and you know that's pretty good."

"Well, I don't know. Maybe I should learn to play then go in that back room and clean that rats' nest out myself."

"You go, Dear. Wouldn't that be the talk of the club?" Steve's eyes shone as he smiled warmly. "Let's go, Kat."

He held the door open for her as she stepped inside. There were five players, partially filled glasses and ash trays in front of them. They leaned back as Steve introduced Chamber of Commerce member, Kat Pearse.

Amy Grand indicated an empty chair. "Join us, Kat. I need another gal at the table just to show these bluffers how to play poker."

Kat eased into the chair. "Don't mind if I do. Steve, is it all right with you?"

"Sure. We'll take Jonathon home. Have a blast. See you at the studio." By way of explanation he told them that Kat was the owner of the Sunlight Dance Studio.

"Sure," Amy said. "My neighbor took exercise classes there and loved it. I think she was secretly in puppy love with her group leader. Would that be Jonathon?"

"Yes. He's my partner and a very fine teacher, too."

Five hands later, Kat was the chip leader. Ed Naples, owner of the local U-Haul franchise, hunched over his cards, face red and brow furrowed.

"I'm raising twenty dollars. It's up to you, Miss Pearse."

It was like he was telling her to please fold and Kat read the signal. She toyed with her cards, pushing them back and forth in front of her. "You'd love for me to toss in, right? Why? Good cards? Or maybe just Ka-Ka?"

His lips pursed tightly. Kat smiled. She passed in her twenty and ten more hoping her two tens were enough.

"What? You're raising? I don't think you have squat." He stared at his two cards again, then pushed in ten more.

The flop was a six and jack of hearts and a king of clubs. Ed sat up. He held a six of spades and a seven of diamonds giving him a low pair. They both checked. The street card was a ten of spades giving Kat three of a kind. She pushed her money toward Ed.

"I'm all in."

Ed looked at the stack. She would take all of his chips if she won and even doubling up if he won would still keep him behind in the chip count.

He threw his cards face down to the middle of the table as Kat swooped the pile in.

"What did you have?" Ed asked.

"The winning cards." She neatly stacked her chips smiling over at him as he watched her with admiration.

"Where did you learn to play cards like that? It's creepy, like you can read my mind or something." He piled his pitiful stack, eyes soulful, cheeks flushed.

"I used to play a lot with my dad and his buddies. He told me a lot about each one of them, how they played usually. You know, the bluffers, the sure things, the ones who made dumb bets on good hands, and so on." She continued to sort and stack. "Then, when we played, I looked for all that to see if I could make it all work to my advantage, and, son of a gun, it just never fails, Mr. Naples."

He glared at her for a few seconds, not sure if she was condescending, or just being plain cocky. The tension was thick, then his blue eyes twinkled as his pudgy face beamed.

"Well, maybe you can teach us all a thing or two, young lady. It would make our games all the more interesting."

He peeked at his next hand, glancing sheepishly over at Kat. He turned over his cards. "What would you do with these, for example?"

She splayed her hands on top of her cards and looked over at him with disbelief at what he had just done.

"First of all, we have a game going on here. You just caused a misdeal. Second, if you're feeling lucky, you could have made a small bet or just thrown in. Third, and most important of all, you don't ever show your cards if you don't have to. If you plan on playing with this group again why let them know how, or if, you think?"

"She got you there, Ed."

"We do that too much, all that flipping over of cards."

"Yeah. Kat's right. Now can we play cards? I have to be home in an hour or there'll be hell to pay."

Over the next few months, Kat became a regular at the country club weekly games. She enjoyed the original crowd. The occasional drop-in challenged them to use all their new-found skills, to read the newcomer. Often, lengthy discussions about bluffs and bets and dumb moves followed the match. Kat hadn't enjoyed this much card playing activity since the days her dad encouraged her to play with his cronies around town.

"Where's your car?" Naples followed her to the parking lot after yet another heated discussion on strategy.

"I took it in for a regular tune-up and they found I needed a brake job, so I had to leave it until tomorrow."

"You need a ride or something?"

"No. But thanks anyway. Jonathon will be here shortly. He's my Mr. Dependable" She sat on the bench at the edge of the sidewalk. Amy Grant waved from her car.

"See you next time. Good night." They both waved at her.

He sat next to her, his bulky thighs flared out, chunky hands splayed over his knees. He started slowly, Kat looking at him quizzically.

"One of my long time haulers, he receives and delivers trailers for me all over the country, gave me an entry to a tournament in Tunica, Mississippi for next month. He got it from one of our managers in Memphis. I can't go. Hell, I wouldn't make it past the first round, but I bet you would. Interested?"

Kat leaned back. "I'd have to think about it, Ed. It does sound intriguing and different. I do have a business to run and a week or so away is a big chunk of time. Right now, I just don't know. Let me talk about it some more with the folks who would be affected by my absence."

"What about Mr. Dependable? Couldn't he run the show for a week? Maybe do some creative scheduling with your clients, stuff like that? You know, Kat, and you can take this from someone who knows what he's talking about, you should run the business not let the business run you. I'd really like you to take a shot at this tournament because I feel you have a chance to finish in the money. All I'm interested in is a token five percent of whatever you win. What do you say? Think you can do it?"

"If you mean finishing in the money, of course I can do it. Taking the time away from my business, well, Can I let you know at the next game?"

He patted her hand. "Sure. But give it some serious thought. Let's not waste this opportunity. It could be fun and profitable for both of us."

Naples rose and shuffled back up the sidewalk to the country club entrance as Jonathon pulled up.

"Hey."

"Hey, yourself. Did you beat them all? Again?"

Kat stared out the window as he turned on to the main road and left the parking lot.

"Do you think you could take over for about a week next month while I go away?" She turned to look at his face and saw disappointment.

"Alone? By yourself? Like you need to get away from us all for a while?" He looked grim in the harsh blue lights from the dashboard.

"No, nothing like that at all. Ed Naples has a free entry to a poker tournament in Tunica, Mississippi. He can't use it so he asked me if I wanted to go in his place. All he wants is five percent of whatever I win. I suppose that's more than fair."

"You realize that five percent of a million is ten grand, right?"

"Yes, but ten grand out of a million is a small price to pay. He's gambling, too, because five percent of nothing is nothing and that could easily happen, too. I'd like to go. It would be the most different get-away I ever took, but I do need you to take the reins while I'm away. There isn't anyone else I can trust, you know that."

He sighed. "It sounds like you've already made up your mind. We have a month to decide what to do about the gym teacher who shows up late and skips lessons on a whim. You've been covering for her, but what am I supposed to do with her classes?"

"I know. I'll talk with her. She has been taking advantage. And if it happens, re-schedule her classes at half price. One week won't hurt us."

He stopped the car and Kat opened her door but didn't get out.

"Thanks, buddy. I knew you'd say it would be okay. Now I owe you a big one."

He leaned over into her space. "See, if we were married, I'd have a fifty percent interest in the studio and then...."

"Please, Jonathon. No pressure, okay?"

"I know." He picked up her hand and kissed it gently. "If I play my cards right and have patience, well, you know, like that card game you love so much."

She smiled at him. "Thanks."

Chapter 11

He went to the fridge and took out two beers, hesitated, put one back and grabbed a can of soda which he tossed over to Samantha.

"I ran into Nina Krepelli just now, at the store."

"Really? What's she doing here? Oh, that's right, she gets the summers off. Sweet." She tilted the can back and sipped.

"Her aunt is sick or something. I don't know. She's such a blabber mouth. Know what she said when I told her about Tunica?"

"What?"

"She wanted to come with me to be my poker coach. Ha." Hoyt coughed as he smiled crookedly at her. "A coach for me. What crap."

"Hey, you could do worse. She's kind of cute in her, you know, old age and she does have a steady job. Just think if you two got together." She glanced sideways at him. "Hell, you could play poker happily ever after and the best part, she never seemed to mind your freaky dumb looks. A match made in heaven." Sam took another swig of soda, looked up at the ceiling and shouted,, "What are you kids doing up there? Get out of Grampa's room. You hear?" She grinned as she heard the steps running down the hall, down the stairs and out the back door.

"They listen to me. Can you believe that? But, I suppose kids are either good or bad no matter what you do, right?"

"Yeah, Sammy, you're gonna be momma of the year, hands down, no questions asked. You're just lucky that your kids aren't like you. Ever think of that?"

"As long as they never pick up any of your habits, they will be just fine. So how about Krepelli?"

He picked at a fingernail. "She's too ditzy. And she doesn't play a good hand of poker. When she beats me, it's just dumbass luck. She has plenty of that. Did you ever think she'd be smart enough to be a teacher?"

"Why not?" Samantha twirled a tress of her honey blonde hair. "She was an okay student and what is it to become a teacher? It's all dirty looks, assignments and picking favorites. Hell, I could have been one, too, if I stayed in school." Taking another sip of soda, she looked over at her brother, stared at him for a moment, then cleared her throat. "By the way, I heard that Mona is, you know, knocked up."

"No shit? I didn't know that little weasel had it in him. Poor little baby getting born into their scary world. He'll probably enter life wearing an Armani suit and carrying a brief case." His laugh was guttural.

Sam giggled. "What a picture. Best of all for you, rumor on the Westchester streets is that they're moving out to the Hamptons. Good riddance, right?"

Picking at the wet beer bottle label, he stared at the rug pensively. "One good thing about this section of town is that the neighbors keep to themselves and move in and out a lot. Most of them don't even know us, thank God." He hesitated, then coughed. "About all that, Sam, you know I never really…."

"Forget it. You're my brother even though you were usually a jerk to me through our whole childhood. But, that Mona, that was way over the top. If it wasn't so serious, it'd be the biggest joke of the Jersey shore. You and Mona. Come on, give me a break. I know you had to be dead drunk to wake up on the beach with that witch. And that pock-faced Philip." She shivered. "He always gave me the willies in school with those fish eyes and greasy hair and let's not forget those pale hands. It's like his hands didn't have any bones in them, like they were sewn on to his wrists and stuffed with marshmallows. What a wuss. Now he's buying a place in the Hamptons. Bet that marriage doesn't last, especially out there in high society. Those people will catch on to their antics real soon and our Mona and Philip will be sitting on their patio all alone. Oh, with their poor little one. What do you think?"

"Me, personally, I couldn't care less about them. I don't even like to think about the grief they gave me. I wish them ill." He tilted his back and took a long drink.

***

Greg muttered to himself as he drove along, crawled would be a better word. He tapped the steering wheel in time with Bon Jovi's *Outlaw,* inching along the center lane moving a hair faster than the slow lane.

He whined, "Every time it rains or snows or the wind blows, some ass holes end up along the railing, in the ditch or into each other creatin' a slow-go for the rest of us."

Car lights began picking up the problem ahead. A black sedan was nose end in the ditch, the rear end up in the air. "Typical," he shouted over the music.

As he approached, he slowed and spotted a couple standing on the shoulder, a trooper at their side, blue lights flashing off their slick raincoats. He slowed some more and strained to see the couple.

"Holy shit. Philip and Mona? No way. Hey guys, nice going. You made my night, freaks." His voice drowned out the music as he laughed wildly. He was almost tempted to work his way over to the side of the road and offer his help. Almost. Not quite. He gunned the engine and moved quickly to catch up with the car ahead. His smile was wide and he felt as if he had just received a gift, a real gift.

Chapter 12

"Ready for a friendly game there, Bert?"
"Yes I am, James. Yes I am. What a day. Do you think crime is on the upswing here in Wade County?"
"Hell, Bert. Not just here. All over West Virginia. Hey, all over the country. Don't you read the papers? It used to be the occasional bar fight gone bad, domestic violence, stuff like that. We really earn our money these days, don't we?"
"Right. Lets get a beer. You ready to go in the back so I can take some of your dough from you? I could use a few spare bucks."
"Soon as old Ronnie gets here."
"Sometimes I wish she wouldn't show up. She's too good for me. I can never read her but she always seems to know just about what I have. She once let me know that I had two kings against her two jacks, so she folded after the street card to save some of her money. So how did she sense that I had her beat? Can you tell me that?"
"I have no idea, Jim. Old Ronnie is a strange one all right."
"Yeah. What's her deal anyway? I never knew anyone, especially a young lady like her, get so all wrapped up in forensics. Me and you, you know, we just do our jobs, do them well, get paid and go home. That one, though, she's going to be the M.E. one day. I get the willies just going into that morgue to id a John Doe, she spends hours there, even puts in overtime."

Bert made circles with his cold, wet bottle. "We all have our quirks. Some of my first cases still haunt me, too. It never gets easier. She was only seventeen when she got involved. Remember that murder in the alley off Fourth Avenue?"

"Sure. Poor Betty Johnston from the bakery. Nice, nice lady. It was the husband, as I remember. Something about the money from the sale of the bakery."

"Right. That was Ronnie who found the body. Ended up being my case, but old Ronnie had it pretty much under wraps by the time I arrived on the scene, down to a description of the suspect and the license number of his car."

"Really? That was our girl? I was working the other side of town in those days. But I do recall that a civilian was instrumental in the arrest. Well what do you know. So that experience is what led her to becoming a crackerjack forensics cop?" Jim raised his eyebrows.

"That was it. There was a stretch of time where she was babysitting the victim, you know, before the crime scene people get there, and I think it was that gap that changed her young life forever. Doc Ringer told me she came to his door later that night and had a long talk with him. She went on to the academy and now, well, you know."

****

Huddling against the damp building, Ronnie Hawke's lower lip began to quiver uncontrollably. She pulled her sweater tight around her chest and stared in horror at Betty Johnston, the blonde lady from the bakery in town. Traffic at both ends of the alley streamed past steadily, drivers oblivious of the obscenity in the narrow alley way between the two buildings. Green and gray dumpsters lined the backs of the low shops. A single street lamp at the far end of the alley, away from the street made a sickly yellow circle of light. Moths battered themselves recklessly against the bulb. The body was awkwardly slumped against the rusted dumpster, head low on her left shoulder, one arm across her midsection, the other resting on a low pile of bundled newspapers, the edges fluttering in the gusts of wind.

Ronnie's head was bent over her knees, waves of nausea sweeping her intestines. She didn't want to look at Mrs. Johnston, but she thought she saw movement. Was it the paper fluttering? Ronnie lifted her head and stared more intently. A finger moved. It couldn't be. It was slight, but Ronnie was sure. She stared wide-eyed at the corpse. It was like the time her mom took her to the funeral home to see Aunt Emma. Her mother stood by the casket looking down sadly at her older sister. Ronnie stretched up on tip-toe, her child-like curiosity winning over her morbid feelings.

As she stared at her aunt, holding tightly to her mom's arm, there it was, a tiny, slow-motion tic right under Aunt Emma's lip. Ronnie's eyes were wide with wonder, fear and confusion. She squeezed her mom's arm harder.

Sitting near the coffin, little Ronnie could only see the tip of her aunt's nose and a bit of soft grey hair, but no movement, the soul of Emma was as still as a mountain range.

"Are you all right, baby?" Her mother drove carefully on the way home after the burial. "You're so quiet."

"Mom, do they ever make a mistake and maybe the person is alive but can't speak? Like maybe in a coma or paralyzed or something? I think I saw Aunt Emma's face move a little, just a bit like she was trying to say something or I think I did. It was scary because looking at dead people is gross enough, but when I thought she moved, well….."

Ronnie stared out the window at the West Virginia farmlands. Her mom reached over and patted her shoulder.

"It happens. There are stories of dead people making a burp, or a sigh, my mother told me that she had an uncle that sat up in his coffin."

"But isn't dead really dead?"

"Yes it is, Ronnie. And in this state, the coroner must be certain that he is indeed burying someone who is completely dead. Before, long ago, many people were buried alive because they were in a coma, paralyzed like you said." She turned onto their street and slowed before the driveway.

"How did they know that people were buried alive? Did they dig bodies up to see?" She shuddered. "That had to be horrible."

Her mom nodded. "It was. When highways were being built across the country, often cemeteries were in the way and graves had to be moved. Coffin lids, over the years, came loose. It was the road crews who found the insides torn to shreds and skeletons without finger bones because of the frantic scraping to get out."

Ronnie leaned close, put her face against her mother's arm and whispered, "No more, please. It's too gross."

She pulled into the driveway and turned to her little girl. "I'm sorry I took you, but I know how you loved Aunt Emma. I just thought…."

"It's okay, Mom. I am fourteen and I know all about dying. It's all the other stuff, the moving, burying alive and all that. It's just creepy."

"I know, I know."

Ronnie suffered a week of restless nights before she suppressed her feelings of morbidity. In the dark, she'd assume the position of a body, hands on her chest, muscles taut, and ever so slightly, she made her lower lip tic. But, the pressures of assignments, grades and extra-curricular activities helped her push it all down, deep into her psyche.

****

Forensics technician Hawke, placed the final papers in a tan folder. Detective Jim Evans waited patiently as she put the folder in a manila envelope.

"Hey, Ronnie, any ideas on this one? Think it was an accident, homicide, what?" Jim had a tiny dimple in his left cheek, only one dimple. Ronnie called it a cute defect.

"You know what you can rule out? Suicide. The bruise on the side of his head is consistent with his head hitting the side of the brass rail. M.E. said that wasn't the cause of death, though."

"What did he say?"

"During the fight, the vic had a heart attack. Probably brought on by the argument, fists pounding on the bar, loud words, some shoving, all that good man stuff. It's all in the folder. Get going on those interviews so we can wrap this one up fast. Oh, and keep an eye out for that mark on the shoulder and the side of his head. Those were two hard hits I highlighted them for you. It looks like a concave bubble or something. It made a deep indent. See what you can come up with.. The one on his temple area would have killed him but he was already gone. We could charge the perp with aggravated assault. She handed him the folder, leaned back against the counter and put her hands in her lab coat pockets. "See you later at the Ram?"

The Ram was a dark lounge, mahogany and glass, a local hangout for cops, nurses and the computer types. Ronnie and Jim used the lounge to unwind after pressure filled days.

"I guess I'll be there since you made this one so easy." He slapped the folder against the counter. "Later."

****

She slid into the booth next to Jim and across from Bert Cane. Jim pushed a beer over to her. "This one's on me. One of the yahoos in that bar fight sported a gold ring, concave on top. It was just like you said. We hauled his ass in last night."

Bert winked at her. "You all right, Babe? You know, really all right?" He spread his large hand over hers. It was warm and made her feel immature, vulnerable, like a little girl. Bert worked closely with her during the Johnston case and they became friends ever since. Just not tight enough for Ronnie to open up completely to him. There was always that silence that she held close to her inner self.

"I'm good these days. There's a lot of work, unfortunately, so the lab keeps me pretty busy. Doc Ringer said that crime is on the increase this year for some reason."

Jim nodded his head. "We were just talking about that. Seems like a lot of people out there are running around with mad-ons and reacting to it. What the hell happened to self control?"

She sipped her beer, pushed her dark curly hair behind her ear and sighed. "It was a long time ago, Cane, and you solved the case. Ta-da. My hero. You were so impressive, like one of those TV detectives."

"I know. We always have this same conversation, don't we? Will you ever talk about it? To me, or anyone? You should close it all out, Ronnie, by getting it all out. Ever since that crime scene…."

"I clammed up. But I did go to criminal justice at the tech because of it, didn't I? Then I went on to the academy to study forensics and became a highly rated technician, so they tell me. Jim calls me the advocate for corpses. That's something, right?" They all laughed.

"I just can't, Bert, not yet. One of these days, then I'll come knocking at your door, promise. My grandmother once told me it took her over ten years after President Kennedy's assassination for her to listen to his recorded speeches. She started crying before the record started. It was too emotional for her."

"I've seen hardened investigators go to pieces at crime scenes. I do understand. And hell, you were just a kid."

"I know." Ronnie's eyes glazed over. Jim stared at Ronnie, holding his drink with white knuckles. He never did hear Ronnie's version of the crime scene.

"When that big Buick turned into the alley, something inside told me it had to be stopped. Then when I went up to the driver's window and looked that creep in the eyes, I knew. His eyes were like kaleidoscopes, his lips were tight, one corner twitching his cheek." She traced the top of her glass with her index finger. "Dad always told me to watch the eyes. 'Pay attention to the eyes, Rhonda, girl. Don't just look, really see what the other guy is thinking. The bluff delivers the most reaction. Watch for it. Stare him down.' He was such a good card man, remember?"

"Your dad was the best. I couldn't beat him. It's like he could read my mind."

"Not your mind, Bert, your eyes. It's all in the eyes."

Jim smiled at her. "So that's your secret. And you are so good at it, too."

"Well you nailed that guy, all right. It took us about one hour to haul his ass to the jailhouse. Still had some blood on his clothes. What a dope."

Bert Cane was among the first Wade County detectives on the scene. He helped Ronnie to her feet and gently took her aside, away from the victim where she methodically described the man, the car, the blood on his cuff, his scruffy hair, eye color, the whole package, a detective's dream witness. But the time between when she walked into the alley and Bert's arrival remained a closed book, except for her comments later to the M.E. who spoke with her at the morgue. Ronnie was escorted to the basement by an officer on night desk duty.

"Can I help you, Miss?" The receptionist was a huge man with a bulbous nose. His uniform collar was unbuttoned allowing his oversized jowls to jut out from between the shirt opening.

"Is the medical examiner still here?"

"Sure. He's still working Betty Johnston, poor thing. I knew her, from the bakery. Nice lady. Say, are you the girl who found her? You have some more information for the M.E.? That was a nice piece of work you did." He came around from behind the desk. "You better follow me."

At the tap on the door, Dr. Ringer came into the wide green hall. He wore a seedy brown raincoat with a matching, brimmed hat. A few tufts of soft grey hair poked out over his ears. He wore his glasses low on his long nose. His light blue eyes looked at Ronnie sadly.

"I was just leaving. Hello, Miss Hawke. Thank you for calling us in as promptly as you did. Good work."

"Dr. Ringer, I didn't really call it in as fast as I should have." She looked around nervously. "You see...."

"Thank you, Officer," he said to the receptionist. "I'll speak with Miss Hawke in my office." He opened the door and led Ronnie inside the cool, brightly lit morgue. She took in the stainless steel table, sinks, X-Ray frames on the walls and the eerie banks of large, closed drawers.

"Sit, Miss Hawke. What else do you have? Did you remember something?"

Ronnie looked around, unsure of this moment. Her eyes were wide. "You can call me Ronnie. Did she, Miss Johnston, did she suffer a lot, I mean all that glass and her legs, they were like, twisted. And her arms were all bruised. I was just wondering"

"No need to whisper. No one in here is aware of us. You are extremely perceptive, young lady.. Most teen-age girls would scream and yuck it up then fall apart. But you're thoughtful, observant and calm. Is it because it was someone you knew, or are you just fascinated by crime scenes? Like on TV? Do you watch the crime shows often? It's fine to be fascinated, you know. There's so much mystery surrounding any such scene, so I think I understand your emotions right now." He put his fist against his cheek and stared at Ronnie for a moment.

She continued to whisper. Her words tumbled out quickly, her dark eyes wide and watery. "It's like Miss Johnston was trying to tell me something, but I didn't know what. Not like television. It all looked misty and unreal. It made me feel dopey, like I should see something, but I kept missing it. That's why I waited to make the call, I wanted to help her, to understand what it was she was trying to communicate. I even think she was like, pointing at me in that twisted position."

"You did see enough to nail her ex-husband. It turns out she just sold that bakery and he wanted half the money. When she refused, he lost it. I suppose we will never know the whole story, that will be pieced out the best way we can. It takes a team to figure these cases out and you were definitely a team player. As a matter of fact, I understand you'll be graduating high school this term. Did you know that the community college offers courses in criminal justice, now? I teach basic forensics there. Consider it as a possibility. You would be an asset to any department. After that, you might even want to go on to get a degree in forensic science. Are you grades good in science?"

She blushed. "All A's. I love all my lab classes. But my mom wants me to go to secretarial school. She calls it a woman's bread and butter degree."

Dr. Ringer coughed and rose. "Well, it would be safer and gentler, but then you'd miss out on all their sad and interesting stories." He shrugged back into his coat, plopped his hat on and they both headed for the door. Outside, a breeze was swirling around the parking lot.

"Give you a ride home?"

"No, thanks. It's just two blocks. I appreciate the information you shared with me. I know you're busy." She pulled her sweater close to her chest, turned and started to walk away.

"Ronnie?"

"Yes, Sir."

"She did suffer. Those bruises on her arms were defensive. He used a broken bottle as a weapon. She was pretty cut up. His last blow to her face knocked her unconscious and she eventually bled out. Her body looked distorted because she defended herself to the end. They do talk to us. It's our job to figure out what they say, then give them justice and peace. Good night, Ronnie." Dr. Ringer touched the brim of his hat and nodded.

****

Jim slid into the booth carrying a pilsner glass of beer in each hand. Ronnie blinked out of her reverie and smiled at him.

"Thanks, pal." Looking across at Bert she sipped through the foam. "So, Bert, haven't seen you for a while. Still working homicide at the second precinct?"

"Still. They send ne on the hopeless cases. It's all homeless guys, overdoses, gang stalking, the usual bottom of the barrel. The Chief tells me it's because I'm so good at it, the fatherly image and all that crap. How about you?" Bert pulled a pack of Kools from his shirt pocket and offered them across the table. Ronnie and Jim both shook their heads. "I tried to quit last year. It near killed me and everyone around me." He rolled the cigarette between his stubby fingers before placing it in his mouth and lighting up.

Jim held up his glass. "One vice is enough for me. No one will ever take my lager from me." They all laughed.

"I'm still homicide, too. I put in for domestic violence but they tell me it'll be a while. I have my counselor certification but never used it. Oh, well, I'm young. Not close to retirement like you, old boy." He drained half the glass.

Nodding slowly, Bert pulled on his cigarette. "I do see the light at the end of the old tunnel, as they say. The minute I'm eligible I'm out of here. I'll have my pension, social security and a part time security job at International Insurance. It's that phrase 'part-time' that tickles me every time I think of it."

Ronnie stood. "You guys up for some poker, or what? They should be ready back there, don't you think?"

"Yeah, right. No thanks, Babe. When you play, I lose all my quarters and after a while it adds up. My pizza is ready and so is the little woman. I promised to watch a movie with her tonight. See you boys and girls. Ronnie, keep in touch, will you?"

"Promise, Bert." She smiled at his broad back as he headed for the door.

The back room in the Ram was a dimly lit office that smelled of cigars and after-shave. Ronnie and Jim settled down at the makeshift table. It was two leftover construction horses from a recent renovation covered with a large piece of plywood. a slick of oilcloth on top. Chips of green flaked off the covering making random circles. Underneath, the fabric backing poked through in worn criss-cross patterns. A wire over the table ended in a single, yellowish light bulb.

    Ronnie's first hand was a ten of hearts and a three of spades. She folded but watched the other players. Officer Wendt was bluffing. Jim had a pair or two high cards like a queen and a jack, she figured. He tried not to smile and he almost made it. She stared at his immobile face. He couldn't keep his eyes from waltzing, just a little, and the dimple deepened slightly. She smiled to herself. Go for it, Jimbo. He went all in with his king and queen of diamonds against a pair of eights. The flop showed a queen of spades, ten of diamonds and four of diamonds. Jim had top pair and a possible flush. The turn card was a nine of hearts. Both men stared at the flop waiting for the last card, the river card. An eight would just about wipe out Jim and give Detective Wendt a huge stack. The dealer turned the card over slowly. It was a six of diamonds. Jim looked over at her and winked.

    Ronnie won the next two hands, one with a pair of aces, the other with a bluff.

    "Damn you, Hawke." Officer Dan was a large, red-faced man with clear blue eyes. "I never can tell with you. I'm just going to give up playing with women."

    There was a moment of silence before the room exploded with loud guffaws. Jim was choking.

    "You planning on telling the wife?"

Dan's partner, Lou, leaned close to him and pushed his voice up an octave.

"You promise, sweetie?"

More roars. Dan's face and neck deepened to a rich purple.

Ronnie shook her head at him in disbelief. "I can't believe that you let a little old gal like me get to you, Danster. Poker is poker. It doesn't matter if the cards are dealt to a female or a teddy bear. It's all luck. Just think of me as a robot holding some cards and making decisions about them, some smart, some dumb. Then just play your cards. It's so easy, even a patrol car cop could do it."

"Ha, ha, very funny. It's not so funny when I lose all my money every time you sit down at this table. You are like a robot, you know. You're programmed to win every time, like you have micro chips in your brain or something."

Ronnie made robotic movements with her arms and neck, turned to Dan jerkily and said, "Do you want to continue to play this game, Earthling?"

Even Dan laughed, his face flushed. "Seriously, Ronnie. You need to get into some of those tournaments. Not the kind they have around here, but real tournaments."

"You mean like in Vegas? I'd go broke just getting there, paying the fee, boarding, eats, you know, all that stuff that costs money." She shook her head. "That's for the folks with the real money, the high rollers, not bottom feeders like me. I just have fun taking lunch money from you guys."

Lou shuffled the cards. "There's one coming up over at Tunica. You could drive there. I could fix you up with a black-jack pit boss who owes me big time. Hell, one phone call and you're in. He'll comp you a room, meals and the entry fee. Interested?"

"What did you do to have someone like him on a string?"

"Don't ask. I helped his kid out of a scrape, wasn't much, but the old man was so grateful he couldn't do enough for me."

"And he can do all that, you know, the entry fee, the room, meals, all of it?" Ronnie looked more than interested.

"Sure. Nothing to worry about. And it's all legit. I make the call and you're on television if you make the final group of players. Bet you can do it, too." Lou blushed. "It's all legal, Ronnie. The guy feels he owes me. To tell the truth, he doesn't really. I just happened to be there when the kid had a bit too much juice and lit into the local leader of the pack. I broke it up, took the kid to the cell to sleep it off, called his daddy and it was all over. But this guy thinks I'm like the Lone Ranger or something. Can't do enough for me. He'll do cartwheels if I ask him for a favor."

"When is it?" She looked at Jim who nodded at her.

"Next month sometime. I'll call him for the dates and tell him to go ahead and sign you in. He will treat you like royalty, no shit." Lou slapped the table with his hand.

"I do have some time I need to use or lose. Sounds good, Lou. Do it." She sat up straight in her chair. "Now, let's practice, shall we?"

****

Two weeks later, deep into a slide of mismatched bullet patterns, Ronnie's phone rang.

"Hawke."

"Ronnie, It's Jim. I'm at the station. I thought you'd be interested, we all just heard, so I called you as fast as I could."

"What? Did something happen to you? Talk to me Jim." She hated to get news piecemeal. It unnerved her because she never knew what the next sentence would be.

"It's Bert Cane. He was working a case in Broadhurst, a homeless guy. Turns out the guy wasn't quite dead, just face down on the sidewalk. Bert knelt beside him, turned him over to see if he had any id. and the bum ups and stabs Bert right in the chest. He just had time to call it in. When a unit got there, they were both flat out, but Bert's in the operating room as we speak. I don't have any more details."

"Do you know where he is?"

"Yeah. General. He's critical, Ron. Just so you know."

"Thanks, Jim. They always say critical, then guarded, then a string of other conditions until the patient is out the door. I appreciate the call. I like Bert. He's like, kindly or something." Her eyes welled.

There was silence on Jim's end. Then he said softly, "Go over there, Hon, sit by the bed even if he's still out. And this time tell him what he wants to know. Tell him for you, then forget it and move on. See you later."

She hung up, braced her arms on the counter and stared at the microscope, the slides, the blood samples, and let the tears wash over her cheeks and down her neck. Wave after wave of choking sobs wracked her chest and throat as she cried for Bert, for Betty Johnston, and for herself.

Her shoulders sagged as she hung up her lab coat and clicked off the microscope light. Dr. Ringer pushed open the door with his back holding a Styrofoam cup of coffee in each hand.

"Where are you off to, Ronnie? Is that a new outfit, again? Where do you get those clothes? The Gap? TJ Maxx? You need to take my wife shopping....say, were you crying?"

He set the cups on the counter as she quickly stepped into his comforting arms. Once again her small frame shook. He patted her back gently.

"What happened? Tell me." He led her to a stool and he rolled a computer chair next to her.

She swiped tears from her cheeks. "It's Bert Cane, Dr, Ringer. You know him. He was the lead detective on the Johnston case. Over the years we kept in touch. He was ready to retire." She pulled a tissue out of the box and dabbed at her eyes.

"Go on, my dear. What happened to Detective Cane? I do remember him, of course. Actually, our paths have crossed a few times since then on cases he was working. Nice man." He leaned back in the chair.

"Last night he was working a case in Broadhurst. A homeless man who seemed to be dead sat up and sank a knife in Bert's chest. He's at General. I'm on my way to see how he is."

He stared at her tear-streaked face and took her hand in his. "I hope you have an opportunity to talk with him, Ronnie. I know he has wanted to have a Betty Johnston conversation with you since the night it happened. It would be good for you, wouldn't it? It could take the sadness out of your eyes."

She shrugged. "You're right. I need to sit with Bert for a few minutes. Look, I want to turn off my phone, so if Jim calls here, tell him I'll call him later, when I get back here, okay?" She dried her eyes, hooked her bag over her shoulder and quietly shut the door behind her.

Ringer watched the door for a while after she left. He whispered to no one, "Get it all out, Ronnie. All of it, once and for all or it's going to eat you up slowly, case by case. I know you measure all your assignments by that first trauma, but it's time to let it go." He slowly sipped his hot coffee.

****

Bert Cane's cave- like room smelled of antiseptic detergent. The lights were dim, the corners in shadow. The duty nurse gave her fifteen minutes.

"He's sedated, but maybe he's aware of people, so don't tire him. His wife left a few minutes ago. He did fine after the operation. The knife nicked his breastbone and punctured a lung. They closed it up and he should be all right but it's going to take a long time before he's back on his feet. You working this case with him?"

Ronnie let the nurse assume that she was working with Bert. They had interacted on cases at the hospital a few times before. Ronnie didn't want to go into a long explanation about why she was visiting Bert.

He was propped up on two pillows, his head to one side. Ronnie pulled over a chair and sat facing him. She cleared her throat. His eyelids twitched. Maybe he was aware like the nurse said.

"Hey, you in there somewhere, Detective Cane? It's Ronnie Hawke, your drinks are stopped, you know." She ran her hand gently over his last two fingers avoiding the iv stuck into the back of his hand and the monitor, like an oversized clothespin, clamped to his index finger.

"I don't have much time with you right now. They gave me a lousy fifteen minutes. But I feel I owe you, so here goes and I hope you hear and understand me because this is it, pal. One shot, okay? My life was never the same after Betty Johnston. You knew that, didn't you? Something like it may have happened to you, too. The way you were so all understanding and helpful, I always felt that you were aware of exactly what I was going through. Maybe when you get better we can compare our stories. Remember I told you that when I turned the corner and saw Betty lying there in all that blood and broken glass, I called 911? Well, I didn't call right away. I can't explain it, but maybe it was morbid curiosity, or amazement at seeing someone I knew in a position that just didn't fit, didn't make any sense. She should have been at the bakery counter not here on the ground with her blonde hair sticky and matted with blood. We get to know the people in our town, like cashiers at the shopping center, the kid at the gas station, the post office clerk, people like that and when we see them somewhere else it takes a minute for it to register, like they're out of their familiar places. So Betty was off the chart for me and I squatted down next to her and stared at her cut and bruised face knowing she didn't belong there. As I was trying to dig my cell phone out of my pocket, I noticed something. Bert, if you laugh and tell me I'm crazy, well, just don't. Betty's index finger on her right hand was raised. Not much, but I froze. Her hand was splayed out in a pool of blood and her finger was up, like she was saying to wait a little while, go slow, stop for a minute. It was like she was trying to communicate with me or something. I don't know if any of the other clerks in the bakery did that but if I asked for a certain kind of roll my mom wanted, she'd put up that finger and say she'd check in the back to see if they were ready. I guess a lot of people do that. But I remembered Betty doing that a lot. So I waited. Then I heard the car turn into the alley. That's when I ran to him and made him back out. I saw the cut on his hand but it was his eyes that told me he knew about the alley, that he had been there earlier. His eyes were shiny and quivering like Jell-o. The guy was distressed, even I could tell that and I was only a teenager. You know how irresponsible we are at times. The guy was real agitated. When he turned around and left, I called the police and sat on a box until they came. Betty's finger was slowly sagging toward the pavement. I watched her neck for a pulse because I thought, maybe, but, nothing. Wondering if other victims could reach out like that made me think about how wasted my life would be if I went to secretarial school where none of my questions would be answered. I visited Dr. Ringer, the M.E., and he put the notion in my head to join the system. Now, I know all about the neurology of after life. So, there you go. What do you think?" Her tears dropped past her chin and down her neck. The sense of moisture on her face made her even sadder.

His little finger pressed slightly against her hand.

"You heard all that? Now I'll have to kill you." She twined her hand around his. The corner of his wide mouth pulled back slightly.

"You were right. Putting that all out on the table did make me feel better. I always felt the need to keep it inside because to me it sounded so juvenile, like a little kid's ghost story, know what I mean? Thanks. You get better now and I'll see you at the Ram. You owe me a game, remember?"

The nurse came up to the bed quietly. "I need to change his dressings. Mrs. Cane is in the waiting room if you'd care to speak with her."

Ronnie smiled at the nurse, thankful that her department was not involved in the Bert Cane assault in any way. Knowing that Bert would mend, that he would soon be sitting at a desk in his precinct, made her feel good. There was no reason to commiserate with Mrs. Cane. She left the room and walked down the long hallway away from the waiting room. Her smile rose from deep inside, like an air bubble in a pond, and spread across the surface of her face.

Chapter 13

Later, at the Ram, she sat in a back booth with Jim. Staring at the single dimple in his left cheek, she felt comforted. Because he knew that her talk with Cane brought her away from the crime scene that had haunted her for so long, she could see the release of tension in his face. She smiled at him.

"He's going to be all right, you know. I checked his chart. One rib was nicked pretty badly, but it deflected the point away from his heart. He is going to need surgery to repair the rib, and they will have to collapse his lung to work around it. But Bert is a strong man with terrific bone mass, so he has that in his favor." She pulled her glass of beer closer, watching the bubbles rise to the top.

"That's great. It could have been worse, right? And it sounds like a simple operation to set it all right."

"He will be in some pain after the operation. He'll have a tube in his lung and when they take it out, he'll feel it. Maybe we should take him a bottle of rye to ease his pain." Her eyes twinkled.

"Hey, want to come to my church tomorrow night? We're having a special ritual for folks who need to heal. I think you'll find it interesting."

Ronnie looked down at her beer bubbling gently in her glass. Jim asked her to countless affairs at his Church of the Pentecost or whatever he calls it. She hesitated, saying nothing.

He continued. "We could go to dinner first then on to the 8 o'clock meeting. It'll make you feel at peace with all your issues. I promise you. There's even a part of the ceremony that is dedicated to the sick and ailing." There was an urgency in his voice that made her grin. She pushed a stray, dark tendril behind her ear. The diamond stud that he bought her for Valentine's Day sparkled in the dim light over the booth.

"You sound like Reverend Leroy himself. Do you tithe, too? Never mind. I don't want to know. All right, I'll give your little church a shot, but just this once, okay?"

He patted her hand. "You'll feel so good you'll want to go back . You'll get hooked just like I did."

"How did you get involved? You didn't go to a Pentecostal church when I first met you."

"No. I was a Baptist. But one of my informants made it a point to make our meets at his church in Newton. It's pretty far out in the country, the congregation keeps to themselves pretty much, no socials or stuff like that. I guess he thought it was the safest place to keep me up to speed. Worked pretty well, too and I guess I became intrigued with their beliefs. It's different, you'll see."

"Well, I am a lukewarm Christian. When I started school, I never had time to go to church or Sunday school with my mother. She did all the praying for both of us. Then when I got the job in forensics I put in so much overtime that I barely had time to eat dinner, shower, go to bed and then get into the lab early the next morning. I still can't believe how time consuming one case can be. You know how that is. There is no clock in the forensics lab."

"Bert and I just talked about that the other day. Like our time isn't our own anymore. You know, you think the day is over and then you get the call to get over to a crime scene because there just isn't anyone else who can do it at this point in time. That drives me nuts, and I can never seem to escape it when that phone rings and I'm on my way out the door. Pisses me off every time. As a matter of fact, he had just ended a shift when the call came in. He was on his way out when the Captain asked him to take the case since his partner was out on another crime scene."

"Poor guy. He's so close to retirement. I think the older cops should have a cut-off point when they are given a light assignment before their duty is up. I hope they give him a desk job for the rest of his time. Maybe he could join you at your church once in a while."

Jim laughed. "Not Bert. He's not the type. He'd probably pull out his gun and start shooting or something because, believe me, this church is not his cup of tea. Anyway, the only reason I became involved, remember, was because it was part of my business. My stoolie was a good one so I catered to him. What the hell, meeting him at his church seemed like a good idea to me at the time. And here I am, a tithing member. It's different, though, Ronnie. I don't want to color your judgment so I'll just let you make up your own mind."

Chapter 14

Ronnie sat in a back row, Jim at her side. "Do those things ever get out of the box?" Her flesh was crawling and she felt cold at her core. "You're all insane, you know." Her whisper was a hiss

She watched, her eyes wide with horror as a heavy-set girl with a soft round face and beefy pink arms reached into the box next to the altar as the pastor softly sang Rock of Ages accompanied by a tiny, ancient pump organ. The young lady smiled nervously as she raised the twitching corn snake over her blonde head. Crooning lowly, she swayed back and forth with her eyes closed. Ronnie noticed her taut lips and trembling arms. Was it ecstasy or fear of the writhing creature in her hands? Swiftly, she bent back over the box and released the snake. The pastor, still crooning, put his arm around her shoulders and led her to her seat where a tall man with scruffy black hair and beard put his arm around her. She leaned into him, her head against his shoulder.

Ronnie pulled Jim close. "Let's go, please."

Outside, she was quiet as they walked to his car. She chose her words carefully. "Did you ever do that, detective? Far be it for me to disparage anyone's religion. I consider myself an inactive Christian at best, but that so-called ritual in there was tribal, ignorant and downright dangerous." Her voice shook a little as she finished and looked up at him. High in the pine trees, a tree spider rubbed his hind legs together and made a loud whirring sound. "Shouldn't you know better?"

He opened the car door. "I was raised a Baptist. That's my church since forever. These folks take the Bible much more literally than we do. They believe in lifting up serpents, what can I say? Sure, we all do it one time or another when we feel extra help is needed for one issue or another. The belief is that the serpent can heal our spirit. In the beginning I was repulsed, too, but the more I saw how the congregation responded to the process, the more intrigued I became until one night I felt myself intensely drawn to the box at the front of the church. I made my way toward it and froze. The minister whispered into my ear to go ahead, not be afraid, the creatures were harmless, so I did it. I raised a serpent over my head and the crowd made me feel like a hero. If the serpent doesn't bite you, then you will be stronger for the experience. If it does, then you are not deserving." Ronnie rolled her eyes at him in disbelief. "But, is it any more queer than your fascination with corpses? Is it? I couldn't do what you do all day, handling dead victims."

Ronnie was stunned. She didn't know that her job bothered Jim that much. A sad shudder shook her tiny body. "You realize that forensics is a necessary part of solving crimes and that many of them would go unsolved if it weren't for people like me? I don't mean to put myself on any kind of pedestal, but very often my findings make your job extremely easy. You're picking up snakes that could fight back, bite you, give you an infection, even kill you. My charges are quite harmless. There's a big difference."

"You need to listen to the sermon the pastor delivers after those who wish to lift the serpents have all been satisfied."

"I don't think anything he says would ever convince me to put my hand into that box, and, Jimmy, if I were you, I'd be very, very careful."

"There was this lady who had a huge boil on her neck. She was in such pain that she could hardly lift up her head. She made her way to the box, reached in and lifted out a serpent that she gently put on the back of her neck, like a scarf. The head of the critter was right along side her face and I thought if she ever was bitten, she'd feel it. But she just stood there and let it flow across her neck, then she'd lift it and put it back again. She did that about five times. I held my breath until my lungs hurt. My stool pigeon kept poking me and whispering that the snake was curing her. I rolled my eyes at him, but I swear that the next week when we had another information meeting, he pointed to the lady and told me to look at her neck. The boil was gone. There was a red welt there but the ugly bulge was gone. What do you think of that?"

"There are always miracle stories, but as a woman of science, I'd have to spend the week with the lady to see what else she did to get rid of that boil. Honestly, the only think a snake on the boil might do is give her an infection that sent her to a doctor who had to lance the damn thing and there you go. Then you sit there, get your wallet out and praise the viper."

The ride home was mostly innocuous small talk.

Chapter 15

Lou stood in the doorway of Ronnie's lab. The far wall was windowed to the floor revealing the autopsy room now dimly lit, stainless steel tables lined up neatly through the center, a row of heavy white drawers along the left side wall. An X-ray picture glowed, a blue-black spine, pinned next to a desk and a table of tools that looked as if they just came from a sale at Home Depot. He shook his head and took a step toward Ronnie.

"It's like I said. The guy fell all over himself to get your comps, a room, meals, the entry fee and anything else you'll need to make your stay in Tunica pleasant. Here are the dates, the contact at the casino hotel and the times for check in." Officer Lou handed her a page from his notepad with all the information written out in block letters.

She stared at the paper. "I'll have to clear this with Ringer but it should be okay. He's always telling me to take my vacation days or lose them. This time I'll surprise him and take them. Hey, Lou, thanks a lot. I have a hunch this could be good for both of us. What do you think? Ten percent of my winnings? Wait, no, twenty five, at least."

He blushed. "Aw, come on. I told you I'm doing the guy a favor. And it will be payment enough if you get on television, you know, those final tables. Then you can buy me a beer at the Ram."

She shook her head. "No way. This is a trip of a lifetime for me and you made it all free. If you don't take a cut, then I'm not going. I'll feel like a free-loader, a chump, you know the type."

All right, all right. Agents get five percent, I hear. So let's make it ten, then you'll be happy and I'll be ecstatic because I think you're going to win big."

She extended her hand. As they shook on it, she said, "Just remember that ten percent of nothing is nothing. Just so you know. But I will try my best. So, we need to practice, right?"

He headed for the door. "Later at the Ram. By the way, how can you spend so many hours in this place? It gives me the creeps." He turned his back and reached for the door handle.

Ronnie quietly rushed up behind him. "Boo."

"Hey." He flinched, shoulders hunched, head bowed low. "Cut that out. I told you this place is eerie."

"You are a big baby, Lou. That's how you look when you get two aces." She put her hand on his shoulder and walked him to the elevator.

****

Across the table from Dr. Ringer, Ronnie fidgeted with her grilled chicken salad, poking at pieces of lettuce and tomato.

"Did you get my request for time off? I put it on your desk calendar so you wouldn't miss it."

He sprinkled pepper onto his bowl of potato soup and crushed little crackers over the top.

"Well?"

"Of course. I saw it and I've already marked your days on the calendar. However," he looked over his glasses at her.

"What? You're always telling me that I should take time off, so what's the problem? Why the however?"

He leaned back and coughed. "It's nothing. Of course I want you to vacation occasionally. It's just that you're spending an entire week in Tunica, Mississippi, a gambling Mecca. I suppose I'm a bit old-fashioned and it is none of my business, but it sounds like an expensive trip what with a hotel bill, meals and the entry fee to a tournament. Isn't that an awful lot of money? It's just not like you, so it took me completely by surprise." His voice dropped. "I suppose you know what you're doing."

"Whew. You had me going there for a moment, Doc. I thought maybe you were going to say we're too busy right now and you need me, or you can't spare me for seven straight days, if I last that long. Something like that. Instead, you're worried about my financial situation. Fear not. Officer Lou Marsh has a contact in Tunica, a blackjack dealer who is in Marsh's debt. Seems like Lou helped the son out of a scrape, so now this dealer can't do enough for Lou. So the good officer had him comp me for the week and waive the entry fee. It's all gratis and I get to play some real poker for high stakes. I even have a chance to win some real money if I end up at the final tables. Hey, if that happens, when I get back, lunch will be on me."

"Are you that good? I know you play with officers and staff, even my secretary, Rose, plays. By the way, is she a half-decent player?"

"I'm good. Rose, she's too emotional. If she gets good cards, she sucks in her breath and raises her eyebrows about a foot. When she bets, we all fold."

He chuckled as he stirred his soup. "So, you can read the faces pretty well? Will it be enough to stay in the race long enough to get to those money tables?"

"I think so. Let's see. I can read you. You have a sad face. Sometimes, in the lab, I catch you tensing up and fighting to keep your face calm, your teeth clenched so tight I'm afraid they'll shatter. It's not the job. I know other M.E.s and they lack the strained stare of Dr, Ringer. So it must be outside forces, probably home, a problem with Mrs. Ringer, perhaps?"

"Enough, Ronnie. Enough. You've made your point. If this was Vegas, I'd lay a bet on you." He hesitated, his head down. "It is Anna. She's scheduled to go into the hospital next week for tests. Her cholesterol is very high and she's experiencing shortness of breath. I'm extremely worried about her."

"Oh, my gosh. I'm sorry. There are drugs to lower her cholesterol, you know. Once that's under control, she'll take a blood thinner to clear her arteries and she'll be back to normal. I'm sure she can follow a healthy diet and whatever else the docs prescribe, right?"

"I guess. We are seventy two so one can expect problems."

"My grandma was eighty nine with high cholesterol, colon problems and swollen ankles. She never gave up her cigarettes or sweets. She'd always laugh at me and say that life was too short to deprive yourself of its little pleasures. I think she could have made it to a hundred if she just followed the doc's orders."

"You make it seem all right. You make me see things in perspective. That's why you're so good in the lab. Your mind is logical. You'll do fine on that vacation, and you will make it to the last tables. I'll be cheering for you."

"For me and for Officer Marsh. He agreed to ten percent of my winnings, if I win anything, that is. Without him there would be no vacation to a land called Tunica."

"That was nice of you to offer him a percentage of your winnings. I know Lou. He's been around here from time to time working a case. I think he's the one with the invalid wife, isn't he?"

"Wait a minute. Lou Marsh has an invalid wife? I did not know that. Do you know anything else? Damn, I practically had to pull his arm to take the ten percent. He wanted nothing and yet I'm sure he could use some cash. I will be upping his cut, you know."

"Ask Jim, he'll know. I am sure she was in an auto accident a few years back and her spine was damaged. I even met her once at a fund raiser for a friend of mine who was running for county commissioner. She was pretty active in politics before the accident and now helps out candidates in her party as much as she can. She's a fine-looking woman and feisty as can be as I remember. Her introductory speech made my friend look like a giant in the world of county politics. So, here's to Officer Lou for getting you away for a while." He held up his cup of tea and sipped. "I have a hunch you are going to come back to us a changed person."

"How will I change from a poker tournament? It's just a game after all and I play it all the time."

"But this time will be different. It's that hunch of mine. First of all you are going to be richer, and so will Lou. He'll use his money to do what he can for the Mrs. and you will be hard to manage around here, what with all that new found money of yours."

Ronnie put her hand over his. "I promise not to let it all go to my head and I will continue to be your obedient servant." She rose from the table and waved her hand at him as she left.

He continued to stare at the door after she had gone. "I hope you come back to your old stable world, but I wonder."

Chapter 16

Ronnie stared at the lush surroundings of the Double Strike Casino and Hotel impressed by the colors, lights, carpeting and jingling sounds. The blackjack area was a bit more subdued. She stood at the end of a table and caught the eye of the pit boss.

"Hi. Are you Butch Lanza? Of course you are because Officer Marsh described you perfectly." She shifted her purse to her other shoulder and reached over the edge of the table to shake hands.

Butch pointed a stubby finger at her and grinned widely. "Aha. You must be Miss Hawke." He took her hand and placed his free hand over the top. His hands felt warm and sincere.

"Please, call me Ronnie and I can't thank you enough for this."

"Aw, forget it. If you knew how much I owe that Officer Lou, you would wonder why I don't do more for him. Did he tell you about my boy, how he saved the kid from a life of crime? The boy was at a crossroads, you know, about what friends he should run with, how to be cool, that sort of thing. A little time with Lou Marsh and the kid straightened right up. I don't know what he told my boy that day in the police station, but it worked like magic. I never had a speck of trouble with that boy again. His grades went up, he graduated high school, went to college and today he's in management at Computers Plus One. I owe that man so much."

"He did mention it when he told me about you. Again, I do appreciate this. It's pretty exciting."

"Hey, where's my manners." He signaled to a young man to take over. "I'll be right back." He came around the table, took her elbow and steered her toward the registration desk. "I think you'll find everything in order. I got you a non-smoking room. If that's not okay we can change it. You'll get your tournament packet now, too. I put food vouchers in there. If you run out, let me know. Do not be shy. I am thrilled to do this." He walked fast and spoke fast, pointing at her each time he felt the need to emphasize his words.

"I'll be fine. My God, the room, the tournament fee, the meals, I feel like I just saved Tunica from mass destruction, or something. You're treating me like a local hero."

"The way I look at it, if Officer Lou thinks you can do this, well then you can. I hope you do real well, too. The competition will be rough, though, just so you know. Some of these folks are in tournaments on a monthly basis, so they will know their way around the table, know what I mean?" They stood at the end of a short line at the registration desk. He looked at her closely. "Aren't you a bit young to be a cop?"

"I'm not a police officer, but I work for the department, in forensics, the medical examiner's lab, and, I may be a wee bit petite, but I'm not all that young anymore. I put in four college years, academy training for two, then an apprenticeship with the Wade County Medical Examiner before I nailed my degree. Now I have six years experience under my belt."

"So what are you, about thirty something?"

She glanced at him slyly as they approached the registration counter, ignoring his reference to her age.

"Butch Lanza for Miss Hawke." The clerk handed him a large brown envelope.

"Yes, Mr. Lanza. Everything you ordered is inside the envelope and, Miss Hawke, your room is ready. Have a pleasant stay."

"Come on," Butch said. "Let's sit down in the lounge and go over this stuff." He shoved the envelope under his arm. "I want to make sure it's all here and in order."

"Really, I'll be fine. I feel guilty taking you away from your job."

"No problem. I needed a break anyway. It's the season for the dumb blackjack players. You would not believe what goes on at those tables. The giggly ones who take a hit on nineteen, or the dumb lucks who can't seem to lose no matter what. Then there are the late-night drunks who get aggressive when you have to stop their play. It's not all roses, you know. You play?"

Sitting at the round, tile-topped table, she hooked her purse over the back of the chair. "No, I'm strictly poker. I've been playing ever since I can remember. My mom taught me and the detectives and officers keep my game sharp. If I go a week without a game I have to go over to the Ram for a fix." She smiled at him, he was so easy to talk to.

"Uh, no offense, but would you please take your bag and put it on the floor under the table in front of you? This is a casino, remember." He pointed at her bag hanging over the narrow aisle.

"Wow. It never entered my mind. Thanks for that tip. How long have you been doing this?"

"This is my eighth year. Friend of mine is one of the floor managers here. He hired me after I retired from the local electric company. I was a lineman for twenty five years and loved every minute of it, because it was all outside work. West Virginia is quite a state to work in outside. By the way, I know your area. I used to stop in the Ram once in a while when I was in Wade County. That's where I ran into Lou. Luckiest day of my life. Now, I'm inside all the time and I like this very much, too. I suppose I'm one of those versatile guys." When he smiled, his eyes shone warmly.

"So, what are you, sixty something?"

"About sixty two, or so. But I feel like a kid. The wife thinks I work too many hours, though. Getting time off around here is not an easy task since the tables have to be covered 24/7. And, of course, someone always gets sick, or needs time off for one thing or another, so we have to squeeze our hours to cover. Now, let's see what we have in the envelope."

Butch went over every slip of paper, every voucher, room card key, directions to the room and whatever else he could think of to make Ronnie feel at home.

"That's everything." He pushed the paperwork back into the envelope. "Where are your bags so we can get you all settled in?"

"Listen, I have one bag in my car. The parking garage is close so I'll be fine and you are making me feel guilty about taking up so much of your time."

He rose from the table, scooped up her packet and said, "Don't be silly. Let's go."

She walked fast to keep up with his stride. A few floor people acknowledged him as he passed through the casino.

"Hello, Mr. Lanza," or "Hi, Chief," or simply, "Butch."

"I'm impressed. How long did you say you've been working here?"

"Eight years, remember? I'm about sixty two or so. Everybody knows me around here. As I said, if I can do anything for you, just let me know. If I can't do it, I usually can get someone who can."

"I'll keep that in mind. I'll stop by your station once in a while just to say hello. Is that okay?"

Butch carried her brown leather bag easily. "Sure. But you won't have too much time what with the scheduled play, the meals, drinks with your new friends and all, you'll be pretty busy. There are eight ladies who signed up. I heard that two dropped out and one got sick. So now it's down to five of you. You'll get together a lot, I bet. Especially with the ones who make the final tables. You know, the money tables. I hope a few of the gals make it. It's always interesting to watch the gals play. You're all so cute."

He set her bag down beside her door and took her hand in both of his. "You keep in touch, though, Miss Ronnie. Stop by anytime to say good night or to have a drink. When you go back to West Virginia, you tell Lou I treated you just fine."

"I'll do that and thanks for everything. You have been so kind." She stood on tiptoe and gently kissed his smiling cheek.

He leaned close and whispered, "Look at this one coming down the hall. See her envelope?"

Kat Pearse tugged at her blue fabric suitcase on wheels. Her bag strap was drooping off her shoulder, her tournament packet pressed tightly against her side.

As she passed Butch and Ronnie, she nodded. "Hello."

"Here, let me take that suitcase." He relieved her of her burden.

She pulled the strap back to her shoulder and tucked a strand of blonde hair behind her ear. Straightening up, she pulled her pink suit jacket down.

"I see you have a packet, too. Poker tournament, right? I'm Kat Pearse." She shook hands with Ronnie.

"Ronnie Hawke. And this is Butch Lanza, a blackjack pit boss here at the casino."

"Nice to meet you both. I'm just down the hall. Guess we'll pass each other once in a while."

Butch rolled the suitcase to her door, waved at the ladies and continued down the plush hall to the elevators. "I need to get back to work, why don't you gals get settled and go have a drink before dinner." He disappeared around the corner.

"Not a bad idea. I need to get out of this suit and heels and start to relax. I feel extremely overdressed."

"Me, too. Let's take a half hour to change from these skirts and get into some real clothes, then meet out here." Ronnie slid her key card into the slot and pushed the door open. Kat walked to her room.

*****

The lounge was as dark as the Ram but much more upscale. Small round tables with black granite tops were flanked with over-stuffed maroon chairs. Soft golden lights outlined the ceiling and the large mirror behind the bar.

"Where's your hometown?" Ronnie asked as she placed a coaster under her pilsner glass of beer. She had changed into jeans and a red, short-sleeved top.

Kat leaned back in the soft chair, her long legs in tight black pants. Her soft blue silk top clung to her slender frame.

"I'm from Knoxville. I own a dance studio there and I'm hoping things will run smoothly while I'm away."

"If you left it in good hands, it'll be there when you get back. Listen to me. I'm the same way, you know, uptight about leaving the work place. I'm a forensics lab tech in Wade County, West Virginia. I'm hoping my colleagues have an easy week without me. Of course, our clients aren't as animated as yours." Her giggle made Kat smile.

"My Jonathan is as dependable as I could ever want. He's capable, trustworthy and loves the business as much as I do. But, still I worry."

"Is he also tall, dark, handsome and gaga over you?"

"Not extremely tall, not too dark, and more pleasant than handsome. He's nice, sort of lovable, I suppose he has some feelings for me, if I can believe him. I'm just playing a waiting game to see where it all goes. You know how that is, I'm sure. You're a pretty girl working within a police department. Bet you work hard at fighting them off, right?"

"Sure. I wish. Mostly I think I intimidate them. No fighting them off, just scooping in their change at the poker table in the back room of the Ram. I'm sure they look upon me as one of the guys."

"Hey, Ronnie." Kate's voice was a whisper. "Look at that one over there." She leaned her head to her right indicating one of the tables against the wall.

Ronnie looked over at Margaret Youngman sitting alone with a drink and her packet contents spread out before her. She was reading each piece intently before shoving it back into the envelope. Her maroon and gold soft paisley jacket over a mid-length solid maroon dress made her look like she worked in one of the upstairs offices.

"That's a poker packet, right? Want to take our drinks over and join her?" Ronnie held her bottle and glass.

"We're not enemies yet. Let's go."

They left their table and walked over to Maggie. She was concentrating on her material, unaware of the two approaching ladies.

"Hello, there," Kat said. "Mind if we join you? I'm Kat Pearse and this is Ronnie Hawke."

"Hi. We noticed you looking through a packet like we each own, too. Got it all figured out?" Ronnie pulled the chair close to the table and set her bottle and glass in front of her.

"Please. I would love the company. I'm Margaret Youngman and yes, this is my poker packet. It's pretty self-explanatory but I decided to go over it carefully just in case there might be some weird rule or two that I know nothing about. This is my first big, formal tournament. I didn't even change from my trip yet. You both look relaxed."

"Yes. We settled in, changed, then decided to have a drink before dinner and the start of the, as you said, big and formal game. It's my first, too." Ronnie signaled a waitress and handed her a voucher. "You want a beer?" she asked Maggie.

"That would be nice. Thanks. Where are you both from?" She shoved the papers back inside the envelope.

"I'm from Knoxville. I own a dance studio there and I am a little nervous about being away for a whole week, if I last that long, that is."

Ronnie leaned over and grabbed a bowl of pretzels from the empty table next to them. "I'm from Wade County, West Virginia. I work for the medical examiner there as a forensics lab technician. My clients do not dance." The three laughed aloud. "How about you?"

"Oh, nothing so glamorous or dramatic. I work for a dentist as a dental hygienist. Getting close to faces is what my dad wanted me to do, so I could learn to read them He called it an art. We're from Bristol, Virginia."

"Hey, we're practically neighbors. Wade is just north of you."

Kat stretched. "Let's hit the rooms then meet back here before dinner. That will give you a chance to get casual, Margaret. We need to decide where to eat. I believe our packets give us some choices."

"Sounds good to me." She leaned back and flexed her shoulders." If I don't soon lose this tense feeling, I may just have to take one of the pills my boss gave me. They're for deep tooth pain, but they will give a person a wonderful night's sleep. He just cautioned me to avoid any alcohol too close to bedtime or I may not make the morning tables."

Ronnie glanced at Kat. "Hey, Maggie, we may come knocking at your door for samples. Of course, I don't know about giving up the drinks, though."

Maggie gathered her stuff and the three ladies headed for the elevators.

Chapter 17

Butch walked briskly around the perimeter of the casino floor on his way to the blackjack pit. The thick, dark red carpeting gave way to a section of wide, black marble slabs, shiny and hard underfoot. He slowed, checked his watch and decided he had time for a drink before he started his shift. Turning left off the marble, he entered the dimly lit lounge and headed toward the bar.

"Mr. Lanza. Yoo-hoo." Kat waved at Butch and motioned him over to the table where she and Maggie sat, drinks and cards spread across the table.

"Well, look at you. Is this what poker pros do in their free time?"

"We can't get enough. Have to keep that edge, you know. Join us? Ronnie will be here in a minute. This is Margaret Youngman from Virginia and one sharp poker player."

He put his drink in his left hand, walked around the table and put his arm around Margaret's shoulders. Her face turned a soft shade of pink.

"Happy to meet you, Margaret, and good luck in the tournament. It's nice to see you three hanging in there. And please call me Butch. Mr. Lanza makes me feel like I'm your high school algebra teacher." He pulled up a chair and sat. "Just for a few moments. I have to get to work. Is everything okay? Are you having a nice stay here at the Double Strike?"

Kat said, "It couldn't be better. The food is excellent and the service is the best."

"Well, it kind of stops at the tables, though. A few of the players are less than poor losers," Maggie said. "Of course, Butch, that has nothing to do with you and Lord knows I'm used to players stomping out of a game without a handshake or a wave, but I guess I expected more in a formal tournament."

Kat put her hand to her throat and grimaced. "She scares the hell out of me when she refers to the game as a formal tournament. Sometimes she says a big formal tournament and I get the yips all over again."

"I hear you, Margaret. We get the same thing at the blackjack tables. I respect the loser who smiles and nods at the dealer then silently disappears into the crowd. Here comes Ronnie and I have to go." He indicated his chair to Ronnie who gave him a quick hug and sat, placing her glass in front of her.

"Stay a while, Butch. Don't you want to hear our war stories?"

"I could come in early tomorrow so we could have dinner before I start my shift. I'll bring the little woman. I've been telling her about the poker ladies and she's fascinated. Meet you in front of the dining room at five?"

"Sounds good. See you then."

He placed his empty glass on the bar and waved as he left the lounge.

"So, this is pretty good, getting together, playing a few hands. We need the practice to keep up now that we made the money tables," Kat said as she shuffled her deck of cards.

"That has such a nice ring to it, doesn't it? Maggie peeked at her two kings. I never thought I'd see the day when the likes of little old me ended up in a place like this and at final tables. Do you know how many players have left?"

"Don't know, don't care," said Kat. "I'm here and that's all that counts for me. I know what you're saying, Maggie, but I can't dwell on it or I'll cave in and start making lots of dumb bets."

Ronnie checked. "One of the officers from our poker table once told me that if a guy looks down to his left, he's probably bluffing. I forgot about that little tidbit until this afternoon when this local guy, the one with the tattoos on both his arms, did just that. I had king jack suited which I thought was pretty good. Everyone else folded before the flop. So I stayed with him until after the second round of bets, he folded. I need to concentrate more like that now more than ever."

The lounge was almost empty. The three ladies sat under a subdued yellow light, carefully looking over the cards in their hands, assessing possible moves, bluffs, raises, all based on the whims of the gods of a game called poker.

"Listen to this." Ronnie took a long swig from her glass " I recently broke up with a detective from one of our precincts. Nice, even-tempered guy, but he hated my job. He said that poking over the dead looking for clues was unnatural, look who's talking, when he wants me to put my hand in a box full of snakes to see if I'm pure, like, if I'm bitten I must have done a sin somewhere in my past life, there's a religion for you, eh?" At least the Baptists know how to have fun." She pushed her baseball cap higher on her brow, popped her gum and shuffled the cards in her capable hands.

Margaret's eyes were wide. "He lifts up serpents? I heard about those churches. We have a few in Virginia, but I never even knew anyone who went near that sort of thing. I was raised Methodist. Mostly, people way out in the country who take their Bible extremely literally, if you know what I mean, do that kind of practice. It has to be scary. I've heard of people being bitten by a snake that the church elders thought were non-poisonous."

"Exactly what I told old Jim. I just got off the phone with him. He is in the hospital as we speak with an arm the size of a watermelon. That's right. He was bitten, the fool. He just had to put his hand in that box, and whammy, he got himself struck by snake lightning. I didn't want to rub it in too much, but I asked him what sin he thought he committed to be so chosen?"

"My God. I can't believe people do that in this day and age." Kat shook her head in disbelief. "I've heard stories, too, Maggie. But from my grandmother. I'm sure if we travel the backwoods we would find all sorts of weird stuff. This guy is a cop, yet?"

"Yes. He claims he used the church as a contact point with an informant, but now I think he'll find a different meeting place. Or at least he ought to, but he's not one to listen to good advice. In his line of work, informants are worth all kinds of rationalizations, but with this one I think he just went too far. You gals have any interesting boy friends?"

"Just Jonathan. He dances but he's not, you know. He's the product of parents that supported him no matter what he wanted to do. He tried sports, the stage, a regular nine to five, but he always went back to dancing. He said when he played sports, like baseball, and he swung the bat, he just wanted to keep turning, and in football, well, he said it was all dance to him. It started with lessons in high school, and it blossomed into local productions, some New York musicals, and one day he will have his own studio."

"And yours truly has the worst track record with men," Maggie said. "I had a hard time in high school because I was so plain. In college I had a study partner who always wanted to do me over, hair, nails, make-up, clothing and she really helped me a lot, still, I usually end up with a string of really good friends and guys who love to listen to me and vent to me, and all that good stuff. But, Romeo, I don't think he's out there for me, or if he is, he is well-hidden."

"Take heart," Ronnie said. "There is someone for everyone. It just takes a little longer for it all to come together. But, I believe it will if you keep an open mind. I have a lot of big brothers, too, and I know if I'm patient, Mr. Right will come along. Maybe if old Jim didn't have such a hard head, well, maybe. Now, let's practice some poker. Let's do some seven card stud just to mix it up and help us relax."

"All this excitement is getting to be too much for me. I may have to take a half of one the pills my boss gave me to relax tonight. That's it for the drinks, though. Can't mix, you know, or else. Now, deal.

Chapter 18

Standing by the large window, Greg watched the casino buses as they disappeared underneath the peaked, multi-colored canopy where they lined up to discharge hopeful gamblers, flush with excitement, hope and money. He raised his eyes to a big sky filled with a sunset of red clouds dappled with lavender and bright orange. He sat in a wing-backed chair and pulled out his cell phone. Before he left Westchester he looked up the number of Nina's aunt and tapped it into his address book. Now he scrolled down the few numbers to hers, hit the ring button and leaned back as he loosened his shirt.

"Hello." The voice was faint and quizzical.

"Hi. Mrs. Anders? This is Greg Guyler. Is Nina still there with you?"

There was a pause, then with an edge to her voice, she said, "Yes, she is. Just a minute."

He closed his eyes. The tone in Mrs. Anders' few words made him wince. He knew her type, prim, proper, gossipy, and slightly above everyone else in Westchester.

"Well, hello there, Gregory. You home already?"

"Don't be a wise ass. No, I'm not home, I'm still in Tunica and having the time of my life and glad you're not here."

She giggled. "Are you at a money table yet?"

"Soon. Probably tomorrow. Things are going pretty good so far. And I keep moving up as these local hayseeds and kids drop out. I have seen some pretty dumb players. Like they almost have a shit fit when they get a good hand."

"Well, those are the ones who won't last. Remember what I told you about controlling yourself. Just try to always look the same no matter what your hand is, then bet your cards unless you can really tell what the other guy has." She hesitated. "But talking to you is like talking to the pole outside Moe's Barber Shop."

"Hey, Nina. There's three ladies here who look like thy might make it to the top tables. You know how much I hate bein' at the tables with girls. Just tell me how to know if they're bluffin' or holdin' high cards. What's a giggle mean
or twirling hair, all that sort of silly shit girls do? Come on, how do I read them?"

She smiled to herself. "I hope they make it to the final table and shred your ass on the way. You never listened to me. I used to think that you could be a pretty good poker bum if you'd only concentrate and pay attention more. But, no, not hot-shot Guyler. You couldn't bring yourself to learn from me because I am woman. Well, like I said, I hope they all rise to the top, giggles and all."

He scoffed. "You're so full of it. Always were, always will be. I don't know if I want to take you to dinner when I get back."

"Wait a minute. I thought we had a twenty bet. Where did the dinner come from? You snorted at that idea when I brought it up, remember?"

"I guess I want you to eat your words over a steak. Maybe I'll get lucky and you'll choke on it. What do you think?"

"Hah. If you don't get into the money tables, don't come knocking. If I know you, and I think I do, you'd still expect to take me out, but I'd have to pay. Right? Just mail me the twenty, okay?"

"You know, I don't think your aunt liked the idea of me calling you. She seemed sort of cool." There was a question in his tone.

"Probably your fiascos in Westchester are legendary, and older, sensible people still frown when they hear your name."

"Yeah, yeah. Very funny. When I get back I'll come knocking all right. And I'll put a pile of twenty dollar bills on a dish and make your ditsy aunt eat 'em."

"Talk to you later, Gregory. Watch your ass." The line went dead. He stared at the phone for a long while before he sighed. Standing at the wide window, he contemplated the distant sky, now dark, heat lightning pulsing. Down below, the entrance, outlined in running lights, hosted a steady stream of cars and buses entering and leaving the casino.

He muttered, "Damn Westchester biddies."

Dreams of poker hands filled his head as he tossed and turned before finally visualizing the three ladies taking the sad walk into the dark beyond the final table. One by one, they gathered their belongings, hugged their favorite players and walked slowly and dejectedly away from the table. He smiled softly.

Chapter 19

"It's very plush here. The carpets are thick and dark, the chandeliers are as huge as space ships and every meal is perfection."

"So you won't want to come home. We have hardwood floors, recessed lighting and mostly our food comes in white bags."

"I miss you, too, Jonathon, and I miss the studio floors and the special lights we had installed. And yes, the food here is good, but without exercise it could kill a person. Now, is everything all right?"

"It is. All is smooth. You're the talk of the town you know, and you look great on television. They keep showing the three ladies, wondering if any of you will make the final tables. You have a chance of coming home with a ton of money. I have my eye on this royal blue sports car, convertible, good on gas, and…"

"Hold on there, pal. If I should happen to come home with any money, it's going into the business. Remember the addition and the lot next door?"

"Of course I remember. But I have a hunch you'll have enough for all that and more. Since I'll be marrying you for your money, we're in a win-win situation here."

"Jonathon." Kat rolled her eyes. "Glad to hear all is going smoothly. I appreciate you holding down the fort."

"Seriously, are you having fun or is it a grind playing poker three times a day without much break time?"

"It's quite an experience. I've made some friends in this short time and the other players are all different and challenging. I am having a lot of fun but I do feel guilty once in a while for leaving you alone."

"I'm managing, like I always do. I'm good at it, remember? Old steady Jonathon will be here with open arms when you get back. Hey, Kat. Don't let those would-be pros push you around. You've worked too hard and come too far to be intimidated by card sharks. Hang in there, play your best game and come home with a ton of money."

"I promise that I will do my very best." She hung up the phone, stared at it wistfully for a few moments, then decided to shower, skip a nap and wander the casino floor for a while before dinner and the evening games. The weather man on television warned of evening thunder storms with high winds. Kat felt safe and secure in the comfort of the casino.

****

The running lights above the bank of slots swirled, flashed and strobed wildly, luring the slot gamblers like flames to moths. Here and there, bells rang riotously evoking screams and air-punching fists from those lucky enough to line up numbers, symbols or bars.

Kat, looking fresh in tight jeans and a short-sleeved, soft white blouse, made her way across the casino floor to the lounge to meet with Maggie and Ronnie. She was early so she walked leisurely, watching the slot screens, getting a kick out of the winning and losing combinations. Leaning against a machine at the end of a row, she was intently rapt with a machine that flashed a bonus round of twelve free spins. The elderly gentleman with the baseball cap turned around and spotted Kat watching him.

"It's about time. Hope I get something big on these spins." He turned back to his good fortune.

She watched as the tumblers spun rapidly. With each stop, the money amount kept going up. Not a slot fan, Kat was, nevertheless, caught up in the moment.

He came up beside her and elbowed her into the end of the bank of slots. Greg Guyler smelled like hot dogs and sour beer. His bulk against her was solid, some of his beer splashed onto her shoulder. Anyone passing by would think the two were together.

"Hey. Cut it out. What is your problem, anyway."

His voice was low, like a hiss. "Like I said, you broads need to go home like good little girls. You don't belong at poker tables like sluts. Stop pushin' me and get out of here. I mean it, you hear?" He increased the pressure against her as he took a sip of beer, his shiny dark eyes narrowing to slits, like a rattler. Then he quickly backed away and walked off.

Kat stood a moment, watching Guyler's back, took a few deep breaths, then arrowed her way to the corner lounge.

Maggie and Ronnie were already there, seated at a glossy, thick oak table with drinks in front of them. Kat sat down heavily and slammed her purse onto the table.

"What?" Ronnie pushed her baseball cap back a bit and stared at a flushed and angry Kat.

"I need a drink." She signaled the bartender who poured Jack Daniels into a slim, short glass and set it on the edge of the bar.

"I got it." Ronnie rose quickly, handed the guy a voucher and brought Kat her drink.

"He said something to you, didn't he? What?" Maggie looked pale, washed out.

"Yes. I was watching the slots and he sidled up, pressed me against a machine and told me to go home. He called me a slut for sitting at a poker table, even spilled some of his drink on me." Her eyes welled up.

"He got me in the hall on the way to my room. The man is like a snake. It's this Greg Guyler, right?"

"Looks like he's making his rounds. You know what I think?" Maggie pushed her bracelet higher on her arm. "I think he is the one who feels intimidated. Must be something about women in his past."

The lounge was dim and almost empty. The three ladies leaned back in their chairs, beers and poker chips scattered across the table.

"The hell with him," said Kat. I need to get a read on a couple of lizards at the tables." She ran her fingers through her amber curly hair then fluffed the lacy ruffle surrounding her low-cut blouse. The wiggles in her chair left no doubt that she was a dynamic dancer. "So what do you think, Maggie? You're so quiet all the time. Have you figured out which one will be the biggest threat at the final tables, if we make it there, that is. God, my stomach churns every time I think about it."

Maggie stared at her cards, fingered the gold-framed cameo hanging between her breasts, her white pullover tastefully snug over comfortable Gap jeans. On her left hand she wore a diamond encrusted onyx ring, a gift from her aunt. The ring on her right hand flashed red in the dim overhead basket light. She had a slight drawl when she spoke and she spoke softly, thoughtfully.

"I think the biggest threat at that final table will be the three of us because we're a new breed to poker. There are still not too many women playing. The boys won't know how to read us. To them, we're either dumb, ditzy, or dramatic and in poker, all that is hard to decipher. Playing for fun like this is helpful because we can analyze all kinds of situations. Daddy was happy when I went to dental tech school. He said I'd learn what people were thinking, being so close to their faces, and all." She stood and signaled the bartender, pointing down at the table.

"Your daddy still alive?" Kat asked

"Nah. He died five years ago, after he taught me all he knew about poker. The man played every weekend at the local barber shop. In the back room, of course." Maggie blushed slightly. "It was banned in our town."

"You still call him Daddy, though ,eh? That's a real southern thing. Mine is Pop ever since I can remember. He's in construction, you know the type, pick-up truck, scruffy beard, long neck beers and NASCAR."

Ronnie shrugged. "North, South, what's the difference? As long as they don't handle snakes like Jim. There were a lot of daddies in that church of his that just stood around watching their women hold those critters above their heads, swaying and swooning like zombies." She shivered.

Peeking at her two cards, Kat pushed a few chips to the center of the table. "So, who looks the baddest of the bad, besides us, that is?"

Maggie flicked some chips over to the pile. "The one who reacted to us. He has the blackest, oiliest hair I ever saw. And he made it clear he wants us out."

Ronnie sat straight, stiffened, eyes wide, gum poised between her teeth. "Damn."

"What?"

She lowered her cards slowly. "That old beady-eyed slime, like a black snake." Her voice was low and whispery, arms folded across her chest in an almost defensive position. "He has a lot of nerve wishing me bad luck and telling me to not play well, not so much telling as warning."

"We need to look at this a little more closely," Kat said. "Maggie, you are correct. After all, what does it tell us about him? He is intimidated by the likes of us. None of the other fellows reacted like he did. He's the one with the big problem. I bet he's Mafia. He comes from New York City, you know. One of the guys at an early table gabbed a little about some of the players."

"Know what I think from my experience with faces? I think he's a putz, but a dangerous one because he sees and understands his situation at all times and needs to control it, but he's the type who won't get involved himself. He'll have someone act for him. Bet he has a buddy around here somewhere." Her voice trailed off, a bit frightened and a tad confused, unsure about her conjecture. "We just don't know what this boy is capable of doing when he feels threatened."

"I don't care. This is so unfair. We need to concentrate on playing poker which is hard enough without worrying about the likes of him. Who does he think he is anyway? He's just annoying enough not to ignore. We may have to do something about this beast. " Ronnie looked at the other two wondering what alternatives they had.

"He makes me feel helpless," Maggie said. "Like, do we complain to someone and make ourselves look like sulky little girls? And if the casino folks see our side of it and ask him to leave, does he tell everyone at the tables and make it worse for us by having all the players look at us with reproach?""

"I hear you, Maggie." Ronnie sipped her drink. "Who is going to listen? He hasn't exactly assaulted us, just cheap talk and what do you do with that?"

"Well, I for one feel assaulted. Maybe he used words with you two, but he pushed me, spilled beer on me and made me feel small. I hate that. I'm more than ready to do something about this animal. He is spoiling this whole trip, and more than that, he could end up costing us a ton of money if we lose our concentration. Hell, if we lose in this next round we go home with ten or twelve thousand instead of the big finish money. I think I speak for us all when I say I'd like to be in that final group."

Ronnie stood. "Now you have hit a nerve, the money. He just isn't worth risking all that money we stand to lose if we let him banter us out of the tournament. You are so right, Kat. We need to do something."

"But what? Every time I think of all this tension I just get confused and feel like a weakling without an idea in my head. I'm with you ladies, I'd like to end this once and for all, but how are we, three girls going to go up against this miserable, aggressive, neandertal?"

Kat stared back at them. She leaned forward. "You said something about pills, Maggie. Have we ever seen Mr. Mouth without a drink in his fat fingers? What was that about pills and drinks?"

Three heads leaned close across the small table.

Chapter 20

It was early for dinner, but Greg was hungry so before going upstairs to his room to catch a nap before the evening games started, he decided to eat first. The dining room was not crowded at this early hour. As he took a dish off the pile at the end of the long buffet, he noticed a few guys, card players from the tournament, slowly making their way along the piles of meats, vegetables, salads and desserts.

His plate loaded, Greg walked toward the two men seated against a far wall.

"Hey, bluffers. Mind if I join you?" He set his plate down on the table, pulled out the chair and sat.

Pete squinted. "Oh, hi. The guy from New York, right?"

"Yeah, but it never got me anything. I still have to work hard for my smokes and my beers."

The men laughed. "Sit down. This here's Dusty from Oxford right here in Mississippi."

Greg reached across the table and shook hands with the tall man from Oxford.

"Dusty, eh? That's a different nickname. Why do they call you Dusty?" Greg peeled a shrimp and deveined it with his pinkie fingernail.

"That's easy. Since I was fifteen my hair got sprayed with grey. See." He raised his baseball cap revealing thick salt and pepper hair. I been Dusty ever since then, over twenty years now."

"You boys been playing poker long?" He dipped a shrimp into hot sauce and bit it in half, sauce catching the corner of his mouth. Using the back of his hand, he wiped the red juice away. Daintily, he wiped his hand with his napkin.

Dusty looked at Greg, his blue eyes twinkling. "Just started last year, on the internet. I'm one of those guys who never thought he'd make it to a tournament. I guess right now I'm just making all the right lucky moves."

"Hey, don't knock it, pal. At least you're here by invite. Make it to the final sixteen tables, and you're playing for money. That's a sweet deal." Pete looked over at Greg. "You?"

"I had to buy my way in. I been playin' since I'm a little kid. When I saw this ad, I decided to go for it. Figure I can hold my own in tournament play. A bluff is a bluff anywhere in the world, right?" He washed down the shrimp with sweet tea.

"I guess," Pete said. "Some guys are pretty hard to read, though. Shit, I lost a pile of chips when that old geezer kept raising after the flop. Remember, Greg? I had three tens after the river, he kept raising until I couldn't stand it any- more, so I folded. I still think I had him beat. Bastard just threw the hand face down and raked in the chips."

Dusty picked up a rib and pointed it at Greg. "Those are the guys that are hard to read. They have faces like leather and you can't tell if they're staring hard or just damn tired. I don't know. I just play my cards and hope for the best." He gnawed at the saucy rib.

Greg nodded. "Know what I hate the most? Lady players. They are just off the wall. They're either twitchy, silly, giggly of dopey looking. How the hell can anyone read those faces, tell me that."

"Yeah." Pete shook his head. "I get nervous when there's one at my table. They smell like a funeral parlor, jewelry jangling, and always with the low-cut blouses. Christ, there ought to be a rule about proper dress, know what I mean? It's hard enough figuring them out without all that other shit going on. Talk about a distraction, and it is a distraction. That tall blonde one was at my table this afternoon and I drew a pair of twos. In my mind I thought, wow, two boobs. It's a distraction, all right. They just make me feel so uncomfortable, like I don't know if I should bluff them or what. And I know they can read me because I'm prone to blushing, always have been. I got no control over the blushing. Give me a room full of guys to play with any day and I can shine at the poker table. The minute one of those little cutie pies sits her ass down, I just lose it."

"I'm with you, pal. I think they shouldn't allow ladies to play in tournaments at all. It's not fair. Bad enough they're hard to read, they throw my whole game off."

"We have three left here and they seem to play pretty well. They're all on money tables, so, better learn how to play with them or you'll walk out of here pretty soon. That's for sure. And with just a little bit of money." Dusty started to get up. "Nice chatting with you fellows, but I do need my beauty sleep."

Pete threw down a tip. "Me, too. See you at the tables, New York. I'd say good luck, but I wouldn't mean it."

"Right back at you. Let's just get to those last few tables where the take is way up there." He dug in his pocket as the two men walked along the now crowded tables. Greg sat sipping his tea. He eyed the two fives the men left next to the condiment tray and thought that was a bit much for a waitress that simply re-filled iced teas. He placed his napkin over the plate, deftly palmed the fives and stood to reach into his pocket for two ones which he placed next to his dish. He left feeling that he had gained a small victory.

Chapter 21

Maggie was tempted to take one of doc's pills except for the fact she had two beers after the evening matches. Guyler was at the table next to her. His piercing shouts at his good luck, and his loud pleading for winning flops grated against the ends of her nerves. His leering stares over his shoulder didn't help. Each time he glanced her way, she cringed inside.

Opting for another beer instead of a pill, she sank heavily into the barrel chair next to the bed.

"Poor Ronnie. Stuck at his table like that. Wish he'd get knocked out pretty soon or he's going to send us all over the edge."

Reaching for the phone, she slipped off her shoes and removed her earrings.

"Hello." Barry's voice was warm and comforting. Maggie closed her eyes feeling a release of tension.

"Hi. It's Maggie."

"Where are you?"

"Still here. Can you believe it? Lady Luck has been with me so far but it's nerve-wracking."

"Super. Everything okay with you? Are they treating you fine at the hotel like Jay said they would?"

"Yes. I am doing well and the accommodations couldn't be any better. Good food, great room and the casino is absolutely beautiful. I've made some friends, practice buddies, two interesting ladies. I'll tell you all about them when I get back."

"I can't wait to see you."

"If you talk to Jay or Rini, please tell them I'm hanging in there and thank them for giving me this opportunity."

There was a pause at Barry's end.

"Uh, I spoke with Rini last night. Seems like Jay needs an operation to remove a small tumor from one of his ribs."

"Oh, my God. Is it cancer?"

"Rini said it's not, it's benign, but they will need to cut the rib from the breastbone to get at the tumor, so he will be down for a month or so. Rini has some bad luck with her men."

"Well, this is not her fault. It sounds as if she really loves this one. He's going to need her at his side more than ever. We don't know how much we need our chest muscles until we can't use them. Poor guy. Give them my best."

"Will do, Mag, and you keep up the good work. They'll be happy to hear you made the money tables but they won't be surprised. Everything else all right?"

"For the most part. I've seen some poor losers, even anger, here and there. One guy in particular is a real nudge. Seems he has a problem with ladies who play poker. A lot of his frustration, or whatever it is, is aimed at me and my two friends."

Barry laughed. "That's kind of old-fashioned, don't you think? Well, don't you cave on us. This is not the time to be shy or to be intimidated by a player who doesn't know his place. Do what you have to do and be strong about it. You just play your game your way and, as they say, let the chips fall where they may."

"Good advice, Barry."

She hung up the phone and decided to hit the lounge for about an hour before she went to bed.

The elevator door slid open and she stepped out almost bumping into Greg Guyler.

"You know , the only thing wrong with this tournament is you and your two twitchy buddies."

"Good night, Mr. Guyler." She walked fast toward the lounge. He fell in behind her then changed his mind and did not follow.

****

She stopped by the entrance to the dimly-lit poker room, empty tables lined the center, a few technicians wandered the perimeter checking wires and cables. At the far end, banked by television cameras and a set of risers for observers, was the final table. The scene took Margaret's breath away for a moment. It was all so unreal, almost magical. She was so glad she was here, a long way from the barber shop games. Now, final tables were becoming more and more of a reality. She continued to gaze at the scene realizing that this is the high end for poker players, to be in a formal tournament with a good chance of reaching the final table where every position yielded a grand pay out. Her disbelief was deep.

"No more back rooms, Daddy."

****

Kat and Ronnie waved as she entered the lounge and made her way between tables. She sat and shook her head sadly.

"You will never guess who just had some words for me at the elevator."

Ronnie puffed her cheeks and blew air out with a moan of disgust.

"Do we constantly have to have this pismire in our heads? There's no room for it in poker. Shit, we need to do something instead of sitting around belly aching about it. We should be talking about poker strategies, you know, girls sticking together against the macho guys and all that."

"Speaking of which," Kat sat up straight, "Ronnie, were you bluffing when you went all in against that cowboy?" She raised her eyebrows questioningly.

Ronnie was quiet for a moment, sipped her drink then pushed her finger around the rim of the glass.

"See what he did? He folded. That's because he couldn't read me. When I took the pot I didn't flash my cards, neither did he. That's pure poker, cause next time I might have to go all in against you, so you don't need to know if I'm an often bluffer or a lucky ass who gets good cards. No offense, but, you know."

Kat smiled. "Yeah, I know. I just thought you might have a moment of weakness."

"I usually don't have those moments when it comes to poker. Instead, I look for them in the other players. After the flop I can get a clue as to what's what.

You gals can figure it out, too. I've seen you both in action and," Ronnie winked, "I dread being at the same table with you two and I have a strong hunch it just might happen."

Kat whooped and the three ladies lifted their glasses. Then Maggie fell quiet. She twisted her whiskey sour between her palms, bracelets bouncing on her wrists. Some of the ice sloshed against the rim. Her lips were taut, her skin pale. Two red splotches spilled across her cheeks.

"I can't stand him." A cube popped out onto the smooth tabletop and skittered across to Ronnie who fielded it deftly and plunked it into one of the empties.

"I get real nervous about things when they're not right," Maggie continued. "Even when I work, you know, with the teeth, sometimes I'm not sure how deep I can scrape and I make a lot of blood. I know it's not my fault, my boss tells me not to worry to go ahead, but sometimes it bothers me and I can't sleep I get so nervous. That's when he suggested these pills. Then, when I told him about this formal tournament, he said to take half of one before I go to bed but not if I'm having a drink, because, well, you know. That jackass Guyler isn't exactly making me drink sodas." She inhaled deeply.

Kat glanced over at Ronnie. "There she goes with that formal tournament again. Maggie, you're making me nervous. Last night I dreamed I was at a table with our funky friend. My pile of chips was dwindling. I had the feeling that the end was near, that I'd soon make a desperation move like pushing them all in with a lousy four and nine, unsuited at that, all the time hoping against all odds that somewhere in that ungodly mix of cards in that dealer's hand, two great ones might find their way to me. All the while Guyler is staring at me with those viper eyes, rubbing his two cards with his plump fingers, giggling at me under his breath." She pushed two blonde tendrils behind each ear.

"He's making me drink so much I can't relax properly, the bucket of scum." She took a quick sip of her sour.

Kat shook her head. "Damn, I better get to that final table."

"I'll tell you what I'd like to do," Maggie whispered. "I'd like to slip him some of these knock outs of mine. Doc said to be real careful and not abuse them or I'd sleep through the poker action. I'd like to crush a few so they get into his system real fast and put him to sleep for a few days."

"I have two kings," Ronnie said as she flipped her two cards over.

"Flush," said Maggie.

Kat pushed her cards face down under the deck. "Shit."

Ronnie shuffled the cards, set them down deliberately, then looked at the two ladies.

"I get the feeling we're tired of feeling this unnecessary heat and now, finally, we're on the same page. The three of us have a big chunk of organizational skills, enough to do whatever we feel it would take to make this irritation go away. Let's go. Get your thoughts out."

"Okay. But not here. Let's go upstairs where I can pace. I need to move when I think." Kat picked up the deck and the three left the lounge for the rooms upstairs.

Maggie sat on Ronnie's bed, her back supported by two pillows. Ronnie was at the mini-bar opening cans of 7-Up. Kat paced.

"The big issue, as I see it, is what the hell do we do about this?" Kat walked to the window.

Ronnie handed out sodas. "Damn. I'm always on the side of the good guys when it comes to crime, however, there are some crimes that are harder to solve than others because they are either extremely stupid in their manipulation, or, done for no apparent reason or motive. We ought to be able to fit ourselves into one of those categories."

"But how?" Maggie crossed her legs at the ankles. "We know the problem, we're willing and we have the means, but how?"

Kat paced.

"Do those pills really work pretty fast? Maybe we could tell him we want a deal, get him to meet us somewhere for drinks so we could negotiate, and then," Ronnie pushed her cap to the top of her forehead, "you know."

"They do work fast, especially if they're broken, then the stuff gets into the system quickly. But what then? Every time we get an idea, there's the big question."

Kat shuffled across the floor. "Hell, we'll slip him a mickey then dump him and his car down a ditch.

That would get him off our backs for the rest of the tournament. Would that work?"

Maggie nodded. "I'm sure of it. I know the pills work and the alcohol would give him a double whammy. We could soak him with booze after he's out and, wow, even when he's found, pulled out and dusted off, he'll end up in piles of trouble. Are we capable of doing it, though?"

"Well, we don't know what he is capable of doing, do we? I think it's a question of who goes all in first and it should be us. He put us on the defensive." Ronnie pushed her denim jacket sleeves up. "If I can watch human remains dissected, you can look into toxic mouths all day, and Kat is able to teach beer bellies to waltz, what can't we do? Anyway, who would suspect three struggling poker gals of foul play? We're just trying to get to the final table in a sport that's male dominated. Hell, we don't have time to have drinks with strangers, we're too nervous."

The three giggled, semi-confident that it just might be possible.

Maggie sighed. "I hate to keep asking the same question, but there it is, as always. How do we get this sack of shit to meet with us?"

"When I first got here, I was early so I took a ride around the area. I turned off Route 61 and drove down a wooded two-lane road that ended in a cul-de-sac." Kat's eyes were wide as she paced the floor. "There were pretty deep ditches along this one stretch. I remember thinking that it was a nasty road for anyone coming home late on a rainy night with a load of drinks under his belt. I wonder, if we get him drowsy enough, could we, oh, I don't know. I can't believe I'm saying all this."

"Don't go jelly on us now, Kat. You're doing just fine. So far, I think we're on the right track. Hell, what you said sounded good, real good. Except, like Maggie said, how?"

"I know, I know. I also remember seeing a restaurant bar type place near that turn-off. I think it was called the Lovin' Spoonful. I'm pretty sure because I thought the name was kind of cute."

"That's a terrible name for a restaurant bar," Maggie said. "It sounds too cutesy for a bar, anyway. But, wait a minute, that would be better, wouldn't it, being close to that turn-off like you said, but how do we get him there, you know, since he hates our guts for even being alive, for God's sake. What can we do to get him there?"

Suddenly Ronnie slipped her shoes on and went to the door. "Wait here. I just got an idea."

"What? Don't leave us guessing. Talk to us." Kat had her arms on her hips, her lips pulled back in a grimace.

Maggie sat up.

"I won't be long and I promise, when I get back, and if I'm right, our ideas might just come all together. Trust me." She rushed out the door leaving Kat and Maggie more jittery and confused as ever.

"She better come back with something or I think I'm going to explode. We need to act and act now. Tomorrow, when we go back to the tables it's just going to start all over again."

"I hope we can do something tonight, too. I have had about all the intrigue and headachy depression I can handle for one trip."

Maggie was pale. "I hear you. But, do you think we are over- reacting here. I know it's a big tournament with the big money and all, but maybe we should just forget about it, finish the game the best we can and go home."

"I felt that way, too. Until that bozo spilled the beer on me. Who the hell does he think he is anyway? No. We have to see this through. A bully like that needs a lesson and why should we forfeit our concentration for the likes of him? Do you know the difference between twelfth place and third place is $236,000? Why should we throw that chance away? We came here to play poker not to be bullied by some psycho from New York with rotten issues."

She punched the pillow. "I'm just not this type. Everything you say makes sense, but it's not me. It's not any of us. We're not vicious ladies. But don't get me wrong, whatever Ronnie comes up with, I'm in. She's practically a cop, so I'm sure she knows what she's doing and how to keep us out of trouble. You know, cops know all the tricks."

"We can only hope."

Chapter 22

"I wouldn't ask if it wasn't important but I need a humungous favor, Butch, and you did say if there is anything, and now there is something. Could we talk?" Ronnie's voice was low and whispery as Butch led her across the casino floor, holding her elbow tightly.

"We can use my boss's office. She's gone for the night."

Sitting across the desk from her, seeing she was tense, he tried to put her at ease.

"Now, what has you so wound up? You realize that I can do pretty much anything around here to make your stay as comfortable as possible, but I cannot fix a poker game. No one can." His expression was dead serious. Ronnie did not even smile. Instead, she leaned across the desk, spoke rapidly explaining their problem, their incomplete plan and their determination. When she was finished, she sat back in her chair and stared wide-eyed at Butch.

"I could just kick him out of the casino, no problem."

"Oh, on what grounds? Three bitchy women don't like him, so he blabs it all over the tournament that we over-reacted, like little girls? No. We want to do this, but our way. We just need your help in getting him to the bar."

"I could lose my job for this."

"Forget it. You're right. I'm asking too much of you and you've been so great. I should know better, this is not your problem. I am so sorry."

"Hold on, there. It's not that I don't see your problem. I do. If this klutz is as bad as you say he is, then I feel, to some extent, that I should do something to uphold the integrity of the casino." His watch flashed in the dim light as he quickly reached for the phone.

"Bernie, my man. What are you doing at the moment? Okay. Can you be here in fifteen? Just a little job. Should take you a half hour tops. You'll be back home for the news and a little richer. Oh, by the way, slip on the black suit and tie. Right. See you in the office then."

He hung up and looked over at an agitated Ronnie who was on her feet and walking toward the door.

"No, Butch. I said we would take care of it and I mean it."

"Please, sit down. Bernie is very reliable. He's my guy. In this business, hell, in any business, one needs a guy. I've used him many times before. He's not associated with the Double Strike in any way. Bernie's a fireman in town and one of my closest friends. He will escort Guyler to a late night get-together, courtesy of the casino at the Spoonful. He will deliver him there, then go home. You girls can take it from there. When you go in, stay to the right and sit along the windows toward the back. The rest rooms are on that side and there's a side door to the parking lot. It shouldn't be too crowded at this hour. Would it help to have Guyler's car there, too?"

"See why we needed some help? We didn't even think about his rental. Yes, it would help if his car was outside the restaurant, but, Butch, I do not want you to get into any trouble for this. My God, we can't even believe that we're thinking along these lines."

"I've been here long enough to have seen a lot of stuff go down and I have been in on much of it, so don't worry. Just be careful with this project of yours."

Ronnie was relieved. "Okay. We can handle the rest. I owe you, Butch. If you're ever in Wade County, West Virginia, you be sure to drop in to the M.E.'s office."

"Right. If I ever need an autopsy. Go along, now and we never had this conversation and I don't know any plans or any pissed off ladies or anything."

"All I'm saying to Officer Lou is what a great guy you really are."

He rose and pointed a finger at her. "You be careful."

She paused at the door. "I promise to do nothing rash, not too rash, anyway." She closed the door quietly behind her.

Butch sat at the desk deep in thought, waiting.

"Hey, Boss. What's up?" Bernie was a broad-shouldered, dark-skinned man with a wide smile, deep auburn curly hair and brown eyes that picked up the reflections around him.

"An easy fifty for you. I just need you to deliver a guy to the Spoonful, drop him off then come back, pick up his car, and you and Jerry get the car to the restaurant. Park it by the side entrance, you know where, and leave that motor running. Whole thing should take no more than forty-five minutes or so. If the guy isn't at the slots by the beverage station, he's in Room 908.

"That's easy enough. What's my cover story?"

The two men sat and talked easily under the soft glow of the single desk lamp. Butch pointed and gestured while Bernie simply nodded.

They drove quietly out of the parking garage in Bernie's sleek black car.

"There were supposed to be two guys meeting us at the front entrance. I'll have to come back for them."

"So this get-together is on the Double Strike. That's class, you know."

Bernie agreed. "It's what they do. It's designed to keep you final group guys at ease, relaxed and ready to put on the big show for the next few days. I understand they have a few more events lined up, all off the premises. It gives you all a chance to sort of get away for a couple of hours."

"Sure. Good idea. Right now the tension in the poker room is thick and heavy. I know I could use the break. You'll be picking us up then?"

"Yes. I'll be back here around one a.m. Look for me in the lot where I drop you off. Oh, and I'm to tell you to head for the tables in the back on the right side, against the windows. Here we go, Sir. You have a nice time now and I'll see you later."

"Thanks, pal. Catch you later."

****

"Well, Jerry. Another job well done." Bernie drove out of the restaurant lot. Lightning flashed, vivid blue and white. A moment later thunder crashed loudly.

"Yeah. Should start to rain in about two hours, I figure." He looked out the window at the sky. "Might rain all night from the looks of that lightning. What was that all about? You know?"

"No. I never ask. Butch usually has a good reason. Whatever. The money is good and the job is easy, stuff like tonight."

"This didn't amount to shit, did it?"

"Nothing too much. Of course, we are only one part of the puzzle. Butch puts it together and I'm sure in the end it will all make sense to someone, somewhere, but, we did our little part, we got paid, so now it's go home, pop a beer and watch the late news."

"Don't you ever get even a little bit curious? I do. Like, why did that gent have to be delivered to the Spoonful when the Strike is full of booze and food?"

"Hey, did you ever think it might have something to do with a woman? Maybe this is an out-of-the-way spot where these two want to get together for a few hours without the noise of the casino and he needs his car to go back to her place, or, what the hell do I know? That's why I stay out of it. I only end up with a headache."

"I hear you. I was just wondering, is all. Funny thing, for all the jobs I ever did for old Butch, and I don't mind doing them, I never hear a word about why I did it. You know what I mean?"

"Like I said, Jerry, it only gives me a headache. I usually just take the wife to dinner with the dough."

****

"One, Sir?" asked the hostess at the door.

"I'm meeting some people in the back." He pointed toward the right corner.

"Of course. Go right back." She turned back to her list of guests.

He walked toward the back tables feeling important, full of himself at this good fortune. It looked a little sparse in the far corner he thought as he made his way to the dimly lit tables.

"Hello, there. Join us?"

He stared at the three in the last booth and cursed himself for being among the first ones. He felt awkward, unsure as he sat at the edge of the booth.

"Just for a minute, until the guys get here. You know, the real poker players."

Kat ignored his comment and smiled. "Drink?"

"You buyin'?"

"They're free. We just went to the bar and told the guy what we wanted. It's all been taken care of. Pretty good, eh?"

"I'll get it. I need a refill anyway. What's your poison?" Ronnie picked up her glass and slid out of the booth.

"Scotch rocks." He turned back and looked toward the door. "Where the hell is everybody?"

Maggie rose. "I need a fresh one, too. You all right, Kat?"

"Sure. I'm fine." Alone with Guyler, she fought off the waves of nerves trying to rattle her. His leer was devastating.

"Kat. That's your name?" His shiny black hair had little spikes here and there. The top two buttons on his black knit shirt were open revealing thick chest hairs.

"That's it."

He snorted. "Guess your real name is Katherine or something sappy like that, right?"

It was hard to ignore him but she was determined not to let him get her riled for the next few minutes.

"There's supposed to be snacks, but they're a little slow putting them out. Maybe they're waiting for a few more to show up."

"Whatever. Where are they with those drinks, anyhow?"

Maggie approached the table carrying a drink in each hand. "Sorry. Mine is a mixed drink so it took him a little fussing to get it together. I should stick to beer." Maggie set the scotch in front of Greg. "There you go."

"Well," Ronnie held up her drink. "Here's to the final table."

"I never drink to anything. When I get a drink, I drink it. It doesn't have anything to do with wishes, hopes or dreams. That's crap. It's just a drink."

"So then, let's show the bottoms of our glasses." Kat took a sip.

He put the drink to his lips and took a long swallow. The ice cubes clinked back to the bottom noisily. He stared at them for a moment then finished the scotch.

"Let me up. I'll go get my own drink. For me, broads seem to ruin everything, like you take away the edge or something. The drink tasted a little flat to me."

Ronnie stood to let him out of the booth. Kat waved to the bartender, putting her thumb and first finger together, signaling the okay sign. Greg's drinks were prepaid.

He set down his drink two booths away from the ladies and went to the men's room.

"Allow me," Maggie said as she slid out of the booth, went to Guyler's table, picked up the dessert specials card which she held over the drink as she stared down, quickly dropping another dose into the drink.

Kat smiled at Ronnie. "Do you believe the luck? It's like we're on a roll here. Everything seems to be clicking into place and guess what? My hand isn't even shaking any more. I just can't wait until tomorrow."

Ronnie nodded. "Yes. Pure poker. Uninterrupted, simple hands of poker to be analyzed, reckoned with and all that other good stuff."

"It sounds so good to me. I really felt that I couldn't go on much longer because of all the stress and tension." Maggie's voice was low as she looked over the two ladies' shoulders at a glassy-eyed Greg.

"He's staring out the window. I think he's fascinated by his reflection and the lightning flashes. He hasn't moved for a long couple of minutes." Maggie's voice was a low whisper. "He's almost out, I'd guess. Two of those doses could put down a horse. We need to act and it must be now."

"Okay. Let's go. Me and junior there, then you two." Kat rose, turned and helped a woozy Greg to his feet. He barely made it to the side door, leaned heavily on the iron railing down the three steps to the parking lot.

His voice slurred, "I have to get back to the tables, got to show everyone, I can do it. Have to do it, goddamn Westchester biddies."

She let him lean on her tall frame as she guided him around the car to the passenger seat. Ronnie quickly slid into the driver's side and adjusted the seat. He muttered quietly, barely coherent. "Gotta get back, gotta get to the final tables, just made it into the money. I'll show 'em, I'll show 'em all, bastards." His head rolled back against the seat.

Without a word, Ronnie forced a pill under his tongue and put the Jack Daniels bottle to his lips. He swallowed, then coughed, all the while his eyes were closed.

"Follow us," Kat said. "I'm sure I can get us to the road in just a few minutes."

"Are we sure about this? We can just take him back to the hotel parking lot and forget about it." Maggie's voice trembled.

"Not a good idea now. He'd wake up mad as a hornet and come after us. We need him out, and then delayed by the police so we can have time to play the rest of the tournament then high tail it out of here. He'll be too ashamed to prolong this little prank and he won't know where to start to find us."

Greg's head rolled to the side, a tiny spit bubble popped in one corner of his lips and rolled to his chin. Ronnie shoved a flat white pill to the back of Greg's mouth, placed the Jack Daniels bottle against his teeth and tilted gently. A glug of liquor dissipated throughout his mouth and down his throat. He lay still.

"After what this worm said to me in the lounge, we don't know what he's capable of doing. Guyler here is a dud, trying to prove himself, probably made tons of mistakes in Canarsie or Queens or wherever they come from, these worms from the Big Apple. I'm not taking any chances on being his punching bag if I beat him at the final table, if I get there. I don't trust his face or his egotistical mouth."

"I'm with you," Maggie whispered. "Let's go and let's make this quick."

"Wait a minute. I'm going to park in that far corner for just a little while."

"Why?"

"Trust me."

She parked Greg's rental along a row of bushes at the side of the parking lot. Taking a pair of small scissors from her jacket pocket she turned to face her semi-conscious passenger and swiftly cut patches of hair from his head, tossing the jet black tufts out the window.

"This way, if the cops show your picture around, I wonder who will recognize you?"

In three minutes, after evening out the patches, Guyler looked totally different. She put a forefinger under his eyebrow and cut it as closely as she dared, pulling his face around and repeating on the second brow.

Driving slowly to the front of the lot, she fell in alongside Kat and Maggie.

"Look. What do you think? I bet if the cops take his picture and they try to get an id., they'll come up empty." Ronnie pushed Greg's face toward the girls.

"Oh, my God." Maggie put her hand to her mouth, her eyes wide.

"We are all insane, you know, but, follow me. Let's get this done." Kat put the car in gear and left the lot, Ronnie close behind.

All the way, Ronnie spoke to Guyler in a firm, authoritative voice, close to shouting, determined to scramble his psyche as much as possible.

"Mr. Guyler. Have you been drinking, Sir. Are you on any prescription drugs? We're going to take some tests, you may have overdosed on drugs. Do you take drugs, Sir? Any idea how this happened? Did you lose control of the car? Were you at a party, had too much to drink, then lost your way?"

Greg groaned. Ronnie kept up her mantra about parties, drinks, drugs and driving.

Forest Lake is a cul-de-sac sub-division of a few trailer homes, singles, double- wides, a stubby mainstream type painted mint green and some unsold empty lots. The original landscape trees, sycamores and oaks mostly, now towered over the park sighing in the wind, providing shade and privacy for the seniors who lived there.

A mile and a half off Route 61 a winding, hilly Lake Run Road was lightly traveled and, in spots, deeply banked on both sides.

Finally, Kat slowed. It was the perfect spot. There wasn't a guard rail in front of the steep embankment. Below, a stand of bamboo bushes, trumpet vines, rocks and fallen trees grew in a tangled mass of nature.

Ronnie nosed in close to the edge, put the car in park and wrestled Greg over to the driver's side. Kat sped off to turn around.

"God, Kat. What are we doing? Do you think there's a better way? We are going to get into a heap of trouble." Maggie's hands were tightly clasped in her lap. She looked ahead, face pale. The quiver in her voice was as palpable as the pulsating lightning in the night sky.

"Too late now, girl. We are in for the long haul and we are equally responsible for this ugly thing tonight. The only saving grace is that I never knew anyone who asked to be assaulted like that piece of crap in the car with Ronnie. I'm the one who feels like the weak link here. You provided the pills, she is doing the actual deed and all I'm doing is driving a car."

"No, Kat. You're important, too. I could not drive if my life depended on it right now. If I let go of my hands I think they'll fly right out the window they're shaking so much. Why couldn't this just be a simple old tournament where folks have some fun playing cards?"

"I think it's more of, what did you call it, a big formal tournament. I guess some people just can't stand the competition. But, look, don't worry. All we have to do is keep poker faces for the rest of our stay here, concentrate on our games and we may just all go home with a good pay day. The important thing is to stay calm and forget about tonight like it was a bad dream or a nightmare or something."

"Kat, there, just ahead, I think that's a dirt road onto an empty lot. You can probably turn around there. Do you think Ronnie had enough time?"

"Probably. She's waiting for us on the side of the road, I'll bet." Kat turned into the narrow opening, backed out and lost traction in the mud right before the road. She moved forward, then reverse, changing gears rapidly, rocking the stuck car. Mud flew behind the wheels onto the street.

"Oh, God. We're stuck good. Now what? Ronnie? What about Ronnie? Kat do something." Maggie began to sob.

"Stop it. Just stop it, you hear me? Instead of sniveling, help me think of a way out of here." Kat reversed, mud flew.

"Okay, okay. Let's think. Stop rocking the car. You're making that rut deeper and harder to get traction

Kat put the car in park and groaned.

"Put the high beams on a minute. Look, ahead there. Is that gravel, right before the weeds?"

"Yes it is. So what? It's a little pile of gravel left over from when they dug out this road. It's crushed gravel with weeds. God, Maggie, what if it is? It's just a small pile. What are you thinking?"

"Could you turn around on it?"

"Turn around on it? How? I might bottom out on it, if I could even get out of this rut to get to the gravel."

Maggie wiped her eyes. "You try to shoot forward. I'll smooth the pile enough so you don't bottom out. I might be a bowl of jelly but I have good strong legs."

With that, she was out the door, moving swiftly to the gravel, then attacking the small hill with sharp sidekicks back and forth, side to side, pushing the stones left and right, smoothing the pile, lowering the risk of bottoming out. Kat watched, fascinated by Maggie's plump form doing a mad polka under bright headlights in the beating rain. She put the car in low gear for better traction, then slowly inched forward. The front tires grasped gravel and the car found safe ground. Maggie removed her slacks, tied the legs together, and began scooping gravel into the open waist, quickly, feverishly, her pink panties, now soaked, clinging to her skin.

Kat rolled her window down and shouted, "What the hell are you doing? Get in the car."

"Right away. Don't move. There isn't enough room to turn around." She ran to the back of the car and spread the gravel into the rut, then moved to the pile again, scooping more and more stones into her slacks cavity, then back to the rut.

"Back it up now, but do it fast." She was waving her slacks at Kat toward the road.

"Okay. Get in the car."

"No. You drive, I'll push." She threw her slacks into the window.

"But, Maggie…."

"Go, before I change my mind." She positioned herself in front of the car, placed her hands on the hood and dug in with her legs.

Kat stared at Maggie's determined face, put the car in reverse and hit the gas. The car went backwards quickly, hit the rut and the gravel and kept rolling onto Lake Run Road. Maggie lay on her stomach in gravel and mud, laughing and whooping loudly.

In the car she struggled into her wet slacks which stuck to her drenched panties.

"He's not worth all this trouble."

"It's over, Mag, and you were great, except for the falling down part. You really surprised me with that gutsy move."

"Yes. It was a moment of insanity but I'm glad it worked."

"Worked like a charm. Are you all right? That was quite a spill. I can't believe you did that?"

"The thought of being trapped in this driveway with that car down the hill up ahead, is what made me go mad and I knew I had to do something. The fall was just clumsy me. I'm not exactly blessed with athletic prowess, you know."

"Let's go get Ronnie." She smiled, turned to Maggie who was trying to smooth her clothes as best she could. "Hey, you know what surprised me?"

Maggie turned to Kat, her hair wet and drooping over her forehead, droplets hanging off the ends. Her mascara was moist and spread onto her lids and under her eyes in haphazard lines.

"What?"

Kat giggled, a low, thick rumbling giggle. "For a well-rounded figure, your behind is relatively small. No offense, but your upper thighs are a little hefty and your waist is ample, but your derrière is, well, it's surprisingly small. Unless it was the rain and the headlights and all. This is a compliment, by the way."

Maggie kept looking at her. "You're so full of it, Miss Kat. I think all this tension finally made you snap.

After all that, getting stuck, getting out, the rain and lightning and crazy thunder, and all you can talk about is my ass? My God. Snap out of it and keep on driving. We need to get this insane night behind us."

****

  Ronnie reached in her jacket pocket and pulled out a pint bottle of Jack Daniels, quickly putting it to his lips along with yet another pill. Liquor seeped out of the corners of his mouth. She pushed up his chin and he swallowed.
  "There you go. You should sleep for two days, at least," she said as she spilled the remainder of the bottle over his chest. The man reeked of whiskey. Putting the car in drive, she stepped out and watched as the dark green Escort jumped forward, plunged down, nose deeply tipped forward, the trunk end high. The car skidded sideways a bit, engine screaming and scraped past rocks, nearing a stream at the bottom, finally settling between two fallen logs. Bushes toppled over the top of the roof partially hiding the tilted car. Steam spewed from under the hood. Inside, Guyler bounced forward, then side to side, his head hitting the dashboard then the window where it lay tightly pressed, the trunk of a huge tree slammed against the other side. He was oblivious to his careening ride down the steep slope.
  "It's done. No hard feelings, Guyler, but you were one hell of a distraction and ladies need to concentrate when they play a man's game." She adjusted her denim jacket, pulled her baseball cap down low and

crossed the road. The lights of Kat's car appeared around a bend and up a rise as she neared and slowed. Ronnie stepped off the side of the road aware of the drop off behind her. Rain pelted her cap running off the brim in silver droplets.

A sharp crack of lightning flashed overhead, the roll of thunder was deep and it echoed down the night sky. Ronnie sat hurriedly in the back seat as heavy rain drops reflected off the beams of light ahead.

"Okay, that was pretty easy. He never woke up. The guy is out of it and should be for a long time. I gave him extra pills on the way and I crooned some shit into his head about the great party he attended and how all the guys thought he was a scream and that he had too much to drink and shouldn't have been driving and that drug tests would have to be run on him," Ronnie couldn't stop talking. "I'm a little nervous but I think we're all right. Actually, when you come right down to it, that was a piece of cake. We really took care of business, ladies, and now we are home free."

They were silent as the lightning, thunder and pelting rain buffeted Kat's little rental car. She drove slowly and deliberately, a little afraid of the narrow road and the deep drop-offs.

Maggie continued to brush debris from her slacks and blouse. The car skidded slightly on a deep curve.

"My God, Kat. Take it easy" She sighed. " Would it kill them to put in a rail or two? This is a dangerous road."

There was a silent pause, then the three ladies laughed out loud relaxing a bit. "That is funny, Mag.".

Chapter 23

The final table of the Double Strike 2015 Poker Series, or as Maggie liked to call it, the big, formal tournament, was brightly lit, nine chairs neatly in place, an embroidered vested dealer waiting patiently as the finalists were introduced. He fanned out the cards on the felt table top, then flipped them expertly back into one neat stack, entertaining an appreciative crowd.

"From Knoxville, Tennessee, please welcome dance studio owner Kat Pearse."

Kat slid into her chair, waved to the crowd in the dimly lit bleachers, twirled an amber curl and leaned back. She took a slow drink from her bottle of water and slipped it back into its slot under the table. Her chip stack fascinated her. It was in brightly colored piles, sorted by value and, she thought it was the most colorful sight she had ever seen, like a huge, silent butterfly

"Next we have Shelly Wintergrass, a third year chemistry major at Hofstra University who finished eighth in this tournament last year. He hails from White Plains, New York. I interviewed Shelly last night and he tells me this is his year to walk out of here with the grand prize." Shelly winked at Kat, smiled at the crowd and put his narrow sunglasses on. His plain grey sweat jacket looked seedy, but fashionable for the new-style, young players. The overhead lights reflected off his shaved head. He wore three flashy gold rings.

"In second chip position, welcome our second lady this year, Maggie Youngman, a dental technician from Bristol, Virginia. I spoke to Maggie right before this match. She told me that she's been playing poker since she was a child. Seems like her dad taught her well."

Maggie blushed as she sat, shot a nervous glance at Kat, then looked directly into the crowd and began re-stacking her chips. She pushed up her sleeves revealing her watch on one hand and a red stone bracelet on the other.

"From Marietta, Georgia, the 2005 winner, Matthew Kendrick, a Department store manager. Matt has won a flurry of tournaments in the South and Midwest, but this is his best finish so far in a major tournament since his big win in '05." Matt forced his bulky frame into the chair and placed his beefy arms along the table edge. He nodded to the crowd and his fellow players. His graying blonde hair seemed bright under the overhead lights.

The crowd applauded each one politely as they took their places and began settling in, anticipation high. There were cheers for favorites, mostly ignored by the players who began concentrating on their chips, the dealer and each other.

Chapter 24

"Who do you think will take the big prize this year?" The lady bartender placed a drink before Butch. They both watched the final table action of the poker tournament on a television set at the end of the bar.

"If I was a betting man, and you know for a fact, Lena, that I am not, but if I was, my money would be on one of those ladies. My problem would be which one because all three players are awesome."

"I know." She smoothed her black hair back and pulled a long, single braid over her shoulder and adjusted the band at the end. "I wish I had the balls to even sit at a table, let alone enter a tournament. Oh, I play once in a while. Behind the restaurant, in one of the clerk's office. Some of us get together just for fun. Those girls are pretty good, too, especially the waitresses, but I don't think any of us can compare to those three ladies over there." She pointed at the television. "Don't you think that takes a lot of confidence?"

"I do. Confidence and nerve and the ability to fight down the fear is what it takes. Those three, win or lose, will be on the poker scene for quite a while, I bet."

She leaned on her elbows and gazed down the bar. "You don't bet, remember? But I think you're right. And, they have become fast friends, you know. They're in here quite often having long discussions at that corner table. I guess they mostly talk poker strategy, or, maybe they size up the guys, compare notes, that sort of stuff. They really have become good friends. You know, the females sticking together and all that. It's a man's game, so I suppose it's only natural for them to lean on each other. They're bonding a lot." She placed an empty glass on a coaster in front of him. "What do you think?"

He waved his hand over the top of the glass indicating nix on the drink. "I think I haven't got a clue as to what dames talk about. With them, I'd say their conversations circle around strategies, like you said."

"Sure wish I could get in on the action. You think I have a poker face, Butch?"

He stared at her, silent. Then he smiled and said, "Not even close, Lena, but you have other talents. You make the best Manhattan in the state."

She blushed. "Go on. Get out of here. They come pre-mixed and you know it, you old tease." Lena took his empty glass, laughing aloud as she did.

"Were the ladies here last night? I wanted to wish them luck but I got pretty busy in the pit. When I finally left, I went right to the garage."

"I am pretty sure they were at that corner table as usual. You can go over and check the vouchers, they should still be in the register."

"See you later, Babe. Enjoy the match and remember, it will be a girl this year." He walked away from the bar adjusting his white, starched cuffs. A quickstop at the register on the way out, a wave to Lena and a shouted, "You're right. They were here as usual." Butch slipped in a few signed vouchers just in case the ladies had a problem with their whereabouts last night.

"We are slowly getting even, Officer Marsh," he thought.

Chapter 25

Ronnie Hawk, a favorite with the crowd received a loud cheer as she pulled her cap low, flipped her curly hair behind her ears and smiled at the other players, nodding pleasantly at Kat and Maggie. Kat noticed that Hawk's denim jacket was a bit wrinkled, like it had been rinsed and hung to dry on a hanger all night.

"Jesus Christ."

Heavy set, bald, Erik Schneider sat heavily, pulled his chips closer and glanced over at Maggie. Erik had a pleasant, round face with a permanent tinge of high red on his upper cheeks. With the proper make-up and clothes, he would make a perfect Santa Claus. He smiled, his blue eyes twinkling. Maggie smiled back and nodded. Kat rolled her eyes at Ronnie who frowned, her eyes filled with questions. Erik was a retired lawyer from Emory, Virginia, not too far up the highway from Bristol where Maggie lives.

"Next, our own Frank Carruthers, a fireman in nearby Columbia, and a real hero in northeast Mississippi. Along with regular tournament winnings, he is a decorated firefighter credited with saving many lives. He donates half of all his purses to the local hospital burn unit."

Carruthers waved warmly to the crowd as he folded himself into his seat. He reached under the table and pulled out his bottle of cold water.

"Everyone ready to rock and roll?" he asked good naturedly.

"Give a good old Southern welcome to Jerry Kemp who hails from Boca Raton, Florida. Jerry is an entertainment director for Century Cruise Lines. He plays most of his poker around Caribbean ports of call." The crowd applauded as the wiry, young man slipped into his chair. His dark brown tightly curled hair was sprinkled with grey. His small, wire-framed glasses perched on his long, thin nose. He placed his bony hands over his pile of chips, smiled at the crowd, then nervously re-stacked his chips.

Rounding out the table was Jackie Lee Yuan, a twelve-year air traffic controller at Columbus, Ohio Metro Airport. His face was long and lean, his eyes deep brown, framed by smooth, arched brows. He wore his black baseball cap turned around. Jet black shiny straight hair lay close to his head. He seemed to breathe through his mouth, closing it tightly each time he peeked at his cards. Maggie held her hands over her cards and looked casually over at him. She matched his bet and relaxed, allowing herself a little inward smile, wondering how Yuan got this far. She thought he was a real easy read. The only thing she thought might have helped him with his game was sheer luck, and maybe the mouth breathing which made him look confident and confused at the same time. She knew he was bluffing the first time he gazed her way over his cards, a nine and a two of clubs. She bet her two eights, he raised, she stared back at him patiently, and there it was. His eyebrows lifted making a tiny crease across his brow. The flops had given him nothing. She pushed her chips to the center. He'd have to go all in, with less of a pile. In ten seconds it was all over. Her eights held and she stood to shake hands with a dejected Jackie.

"Nice job, lady. Maybe next time will be my turn, right?"

"Sure."

He hugged her and shook hands around the table, bidding everyone, goodbye and good luck.

****

Ronnie glanced out the window at the next flash of iridescent lightning. "Hand me my purse back here. My hands smell like Jack Daniels. I think I have a wipe or two in there."

"Is everyone okay?" asked Kat as she drove carefully around the sharp curves.

"No, we are not okay and probably never will be again. Do you realize that we not only took a player out of the tournament, but we jeopardized his life as well? I know it's too late for tears and he asked for it and all that and I agree, but, still, what we did could put us in jail for quite a while. Am I right, Officer Hawke? What's your take on this whole scenario?"

"Look. I am in this all the way just like you two and even though I am considered an officer of the court, I know that what we did was the right thing to do under the circumstances. The big thing, and I can't stress this enough, is that we did it clean. There is no way to trace any of this back to us. I did ask Butch for some help but he wouldn't rat us out if they threatened to pull out his manicured nails one by one. And Guyler, what's he going to remember about this night except he got drunk and ended up in a ditch? Even if he does hazily try to put something together in his weak little mind, I doubt very much that he would ever admit to getting done in by three broads like us. He'll spend months thinking it was this or that scenario, like he was drinking with the guys, had too much and drove into nowhere, or was it the three of us that put him in his car and drove him into a ditch, or did he dream it all. The guy's not too swift, you know. Anyhow, that's how I see it. If the three of us keep our yappers shut until it's story time for our grandkids, there shouldn't be a problem, ever. Another plus, now that you bring up the officers of the law, how much time do you really think these cops are going to spend on what looks like a casino based drunk who ends up in a ditch? I will tell you. About a half hour, then the report goes in a folder that ends up on the bottom of a pile on a desk in a far corner. They're stretched thin usually and they tend to concentrate on more high profile, serious cases. Hey, do I smell like whiskey?"

"You're probably right. Don't mind me. I tend to overreact, as I said. You don't smell too bad. It's the rain. When you get wet, it tends to heighten the odors. I'm probably the one who is filling this car with a Mississippi mud stench, right Kat?"

Kat shook her head yes with vigor. "You would have been so proud of our Maggie tonight. She moved into action so fast, I thought she snapped. We got stuck back there. When I tried to turn around, there was a rut and I kept rocking the car back and forth but Maggie spotted a pile of gravel which she ran to and smoothed out with her feet then she took off her pants and used them like a bag to gather gravel and pour it into the rut, then she's in her panties and pushes the car which gets us out of the rut but she falls flat out, all this in the rain, lightning and thunder." She stopped her rush of words, ending in a sob.

Ronnie was quiet for a moment, then said, "You took off your pants? Did you ever think that there might have been a snake in those weeds? What were you thinking?"

"We were stuck. It was the only thing I could think to do. Goddamit. It was the only thing."

"But there could have been a snake."

"Enough already with the snakes. There weren't any, just rain and mud and ruts."

Kat used the back of her hand to wipe her eyes, then let go of a soft giggle. "Hey, Ronnie. Know what?"

"Don't you dare, Kat. It's not nice to talk about someone who just saved our asses."

"Speaking of which, Maggie here has a surprisingly small behind. In wet panties it looks extremely tiny."

"Really? But Maggie, that's good. You do appear to be well-rounded usually. You should wear more clingy skirts and slacks then."

"Right. Then my tummy would look like a bread basket. I like the clothes that cover all my sins and that's enough on the subject, please and thank you. What are you, anyway, a fashion cop?"

"No, but Dr. Ringer, my boss, compliments me on my clothes. I like to dress nice on the job. I don't have to, but my job could be depressing sometime, so a cute outfit makes me feel good."

As they approached the main highway, Kat said, "I've been thinking. We're in this tournament pretty deep now, wouldn't you say?" They laughed nervously.

"Yes, we are. Pretty damn deep after tonight. What's on your mind?" Ronnie forced the used wipe out a narrow slit in the lowered window.

Maggie hunched up her shoulders and squeezed her face. "Oh, oh. I know this one. Kat, I can read you, I really can."

"What? Can you be that good from watching faces with their jaws dropped open?"

This new line of thought gave the girls the breather they needed after the tensions and anxieties of the evening. They instantly became alert and tentative, trying to stay on top of this latest turn of events, these new thoughts. It was an interesting and welcome challenge.

"You'd be surprised at how sharp I can become when my mind is clear and in focus. I can tell just what a patient is thinking by watching his eyebrows, his blinking or squeezing his eyes shut. There are a lot of clues out there just waiting to be read."

"Okay. So tell me what I'm thinking, smarty pants."

Ronnie leaned forward and put her arms along the back of the seat. "If you were holding a snake over your head with that look on your face, Kat, you'd be silently asking for help." Her voice became and imitative high pitch. "For God's sake, take this thing away before I crap my pants."

The three, once again, laughed aloud.

Maggie peeked over at Kat. "Here it is then and if I'm wrong, then just tell me what's on your mind and we can move on. The three of us should play together, split whatever, right? That way we have more of a solid bond of trust. Right? We would be more inclined to think of the other two if one of us was tempted to talk too much. That's what I think."

Kat smiled. "I bow to your talent of perception. It was exactly what I wanted to express."

Ronnie quickly said, "I'm in. Are we all agreed then? Even if I have all confidence that the moment will never come up, I do think it's a good idea. Of course, we should look at the one who will win the most. That person will have to take a hit. For instance, if Kat wins five, I win ten and Maggie wins fifteen, the grand total is thirty. That divided by three is ten. That's good for Kat, okay for me, but Maggie steps backwards. Would everyone be okay with that? If not, now is the time to say no to the whole idea."

"If it keeps us quiet, and I think it will, then we should do it. Right now we don't know how this tournament is going to turn out." Maggie was thoughtful. "But, if we should happen to end up real high, then it wouldn't matter, would it? We would all be going home with a nice chunk of change and if cost me a few thousand for peace of mind, well, I for one think it's well worth it."

"Of course, I agree because mainly it was my idea. That is before you two took it and ran with it. I just hope that's all the grand talking we all do about this subject from hell." Kat turned onto the highway, now slick with rain and lights reflecting off shiny cars.

****

The eight remaining players leaned back, took sips of water and chatted quietly as a new dealer, a broad-shouldered gentleman with a black goatee rapidly shuffled, fanned and stacked the cards, then swiftly shot cards around the table to each player.

The next two rounds of play went quickly with the fireman, Frank Carruthers going all in on the store manager Matt Kendrick who drew a suited Ace, queen of clubs against Frank's two eights. Jerry Kemp joined in with a King of diamonds and a ten of hearts. The flop gave Matt two more hearts and hope, but the street served up another eight for Frank, and after the river showed a six of clubs, Matt Kendrick was gone, quietly vanishing behind the bank of cameras into the dark. The crowd cheered their hero for a job well done.

The next hand gave Carruthers two queens. Everyone folded except Jerry Kemp who his raised his pair of jacks. Frank quickly went all in against Jerry's short stack. The flop looked like a telephone number, no face cards, and no help to either player. The street continued the trend with the river an Ace. Frank's queens held and he reached across the table to shake a dejected Jerry Kemp's hand.

Each dropout raised the winnings for the girls as they moved up in rank. They were now at least sixth, fifth, and fourth. Their glances at each other were accompanied by wide grins.

****

The sign on the door said Chief of Security, Mike Rossy. He knocked and went in.

"Hi. I'm Grady. They have me overseeing the poker tournament this year." Tom Grady was a tall, thin elderly gentleman with horn-rimmed glasses, a thin, white face and hair to match. His eyes were a soft blue, his smile was warm and wide.

Mike Rossy came from behind his desk to shake hands. Nick was a broad- chested, black man with a shaved head, thick thighs and wide shoulders. His presence exuded a no-nonsense attitude.

"Sure, Mr. Grady. Glad to have you on board. Everything under control? I understand the payouts are extra huge this year."

"The best yet. Double Strike has been very generous, plus sponsors and entries really built the amounts at the money tables."

"Well, it's good publicity for everyone. Are the players behaving themselves? I'm sorry I haven't had the time to watch the tournament, but they keep me pretty busy here with all the day-to-day stuff. Now that we're getting down to the wire, I'll have to use one of the monitors for watching the action."

"Everyone is doing fine. Oh, we have some poor losers, but the extent of their negativity is failure to shake hands as they leave, petty stuff like that. But I do have one problem maybe you can help me solve."

"Shoot. Anything I can do to make your job easier, I'll do it."

"We have a player who made it to a money table. If he loses every hand, he still finishes in the twelve spot and we're going to owe him his winnings, about ten grand."

"Okay. I heard that's how it works. So, what's the problem?"

"He's missing. He's never been late, now he's not even at the table. We will put in his blinds until his chips are gone, then we'll owe him a check. I was wondering if maybe you could locate him for me."

"I'll go up to his room now and let you know what I find. Maybe he's sleeping one off. It's been known to happen. Let me see what I can find, Mr. Grady."

"I would appreciate it. I hate loose ends. He belongs in the empty seat and I need to know why he's not there. I'll be floating around the tables all afternoon if you need me and thanks for anything you can do."

Mike let himself into Greg Guyler's room with a master key card. He noticed that the bed was made, but the maid service hadn't reached this far down the hall as yet. Guyler hadn't slept in his room last night.

He poked around in drawers, the bathroom counter, the closet and found nothing out of the ordinary. Using his safe key, he opened the box in the closet wall and found a money clip with a few hundred dollars, a pair of sunglasses and slot vouchers for over eight hundred dollars. He re-locked the safe and left the room, pulling the door shut firmly.

In the poker hall, Mike motioned to Grady with his chin. Grady joined him at the edge of the room.

"Nothing, man. Room's clean as a whistle. He didn't sleep there last night so I'd guess he pulled an all-night binge somewhere, maybe in someone's room, a dame, you know. Too much to drink, like that. Probably sleeping it off somewhere. I'll keep my eye on our screens and if I spot him, I'll let you know. You just need to tell me generally what he looks like."

Grady thought a moment. "He has jet black hair that's spiked here and there. He's stocky, about your height and his face is round, young looking, like a teenager, but you know right away that he's about thirty five or so. That's about all I remember about him. That spiky hair should be your first clue."

"I'll track the casino floor and see if he shows up."

"That's all you can do, I suppose. I've given the dealers the go-ahead to play out his stack on the blinds. When it's gone, it's gone. Whatever we owe him, we'll settle with him. It would be better if he shows up to play so he can go a little further up the money ladder. But, what can we do? Hey, Mike, thanks a lot. I appreciate it."

"It's my job and it's not a problem. If I hear anything, I'll let you know."

****

Kat had the windshield wipers on high. They slapped huge lines of water away from the window, but the visibility was still low. She drove slowly through the heavy rain.

"By the way," Ronnie said as she fussed with an object in the back seat, "you know that bridge that we go over before we get to the hotel? Well go slow there because I need to toss this into the river." She held up Guyler's wallet, registration and insurance card neatly tucked into the now empty money flap. "Six hundred and forty, two hundred and ten apiece and an extra ten to Kat for driving."

Maggie sighed. "Now robbery on top of everything else. Will this evening ever end?"

Kat drove slowly watching closely for the ramp to the casinos. "So if we finish in the last spots, we split the total of our winnings? Should we write it up and sign something to that effect?"

"I don't think we should go that far. Let's just shake on it and pretend we're card players from the old West." Ronnie put her hand across the front seat. Maggie and Kat put a hand on top of hers.

"Does this make us, like, oh, I don't know. If it was the old West we would be men. Ladies didn't play poker, remember?" Maggie asked.

"Don't be silly. Ladies can swear to stuff, too. This is good enough for me. I only hope we can last to make the winnings worth all this crap."

"Wouldn't that be nice, but, yeah, no matter how it plays out, we're all bound to walk away with more than the tourney cost, right?" Kat slowed as she approached the bridge. Near the middle there was a space to pull over. Traffic was light. They waited until cars were visible at either end but far enough away for them to be noticed. Kat hit the light switch and they sat in darkness. Lights from the stanchions along the bridge were dim in the downpour. The casino's neon reflected off the river.

Ronnie leaned out the back window and hurled the wallet over the rail and into the muddy Mississippi River. It arced beautifully, catching the street lights as it smoothly dipped and fell into the river with a tiny splash.

"Now, when they find the little lizard, they won't know who the hell he is. He'll end up in the hospital drying out, then he'll get charged with drunken driving, no license, and so on. It will take a while."

"By then we'll be out of Dodge."

****

High in the branches of a loblolly pine, two tree spiders faced each other, defiantly defending their territories on the rough-barked branch. Each one began slowly rubbing its long, strong back legs together. The resulting sound began as a low, eerie hum that rose in pitch and exploded into a tympani of reverberating, strident notes. One moved backward and their little tiff was over. It would be repeated over and over through the night as the critters moved from limb to limb, meeting other spiders and squaring off to claim a piece of branch where mites lived under the bark, juicy snacks for the hungry, noisy combatants.

He stood with his legs apart, his right hand resting on his holster. The other officer looked too young to be in uniform, a uniform trim and neat, his shoes shined and knife-like creases in his pants. He stood at the edge of the road staring down the slope at the little car tilted precariously on its side in a mesh of bushes and trees. The rain had stopped and tree spiders and crickets raised a noisy ruckus. The lights from their patrol cars twirled red and blue against the tall, dark trees. Shafts of orange glow from the sunset streaked through the high branches.

"So who called it in?"

"The Bensons. They went out to dinner and on the way home, Mrs. Benson noticed a lot of mud and gravel in the road by that turn off where the road crews parked their equipment. She made him stop by the turn in."

"Why?"

"Because she said it looked out of the ordinary. You know how elderly folks are. If one little thing changes, it's like the universe is shifting or something. Actually, she thought that someone might be stuck in there."

The young officer nodded. "I know exactly what you mean. They know stuff, too. Like my grandma. I swear she knows what I'm thinking sometimes."

"Well, anyway, they turned around and followed the muddy tracks back to here. Mr. Benson said it looked like this guy really got hung up back there making ruts all over that turn-off. Then they spotted the car. After shouting for a few minutes, they heard a low moan, got on their cell immediately and I was the closest, so I shot right over here."

"So you took their statements and called for backup."

"Standard procedure in this type of situation. Now, call Moe's Towing so we can get this heap out of the woods."

"I think we should call for an ambulance, too, in case that guy down there is hurt seriously."

"Whatever. Go ahead, make the calls. I'm going to the turn-off and have a look-see at the action in that area. I'll add it to the report."

The tow truck arrived first. The driver scrambled down the hill to the car, hooked it up to a winch and started the control, slowly inching the car up the hill, out of the brambles, dragging twigs, mud and pine needle clumps along with it.

"Hey, Officer. Give me a hand with this, will you? Two of us should be able to tip that thing down on all its wheels. It'll be easier for me to clear the top of the hill."

The cop hesitated. "I need to do some traffic control here. You are blocking most of the road."

Moe looked left and right, up and down the road. "Traffic control? You're kidding, right? Anyone comes along, they can wait. This is a rubbernecker's dream. Maybe they would even enjoy helping."

He joined the driver and they gingerly walked sideways down the slippery hill to the car.

"Okay, I'll take the front, you stay here by the trunk. When I say three, give her a good shove. It should topple, no trouble."

The officer tried to peer into the car but he was at the trunk end and the car was teetering. He stretched up to look into the back window, but saw nothing.

It hit the ground hard, bounced a bit, then settled into the forest floor. The trip to the top was smooth. Guyler was jammed against the passenger side door.

"You want to get him out of the car while I get this thing ready to tow back to the garage? Then I'll be out of your way and the turnpike here will be clear for traffic."

"Don't be a wise ass. Give me a hand getting him out."

He went to his trunk, took out a grey blanket and spread it next to the car. Taking a corner, he wiped each shoe carefully, trying to get back the luster.

"You're a real fashion plate, you know. Here's the receipt for the car. When Sleeping Beauty there wakes up, give it to him."

He returned to the trunk for the two orange cones which he placed near the blanket. The second officer pulled in behind the prone Guyler.

"That was fast. Any trouble getting the car out?"

"No. He pulled it up pretty quickly. I can't believe the ambulance isn't here yet."

"The station's on the other side of town, remember. They'll be here soon enough."

The two officers stared down at the disheveled Greg Guyler, lying on the side of the road, reeking of alcohol, dirty, weak and disoriented. His forehead was bleeding from a sharp bump and cut. One of his eyes was swollen shut, a thin slit caked with dried blood and dirt. A red welt spread across the bridge of his nose.

"Did you find anything at the turn-off?"

"Only a hell of a lot of mud and gravel. He did have a hard time like old man Benson said. It looks like he tried to turn around but got hung up in a rut. My guess is that after a lot of tries he shot out of there mad as a hornet, started to speed up that little rise, then lost control and there you go."

A wind rustled through the tree tops bringing with it the distant scream of a siren. The bright blue and white flashing lights strobed off the trees and bushes, now darkened by the setting of the sun.

"You'll be all right, man. The EMTs will be here soon." The young officer looked up at his partner. "He's drunk as a skunk and smells like one, too. The guy's pretty banged up from that dive into the ditch." He rifled through Guyler's pockets. "No identification of any kind. There wasn't anything in the car, either. What do you think?"

"Write your report. The hospital will get him tonight, treat him for whatever, then we'll take it from there. He's probably the victim of an event where he had too much to drink, drove out here, got lost, whatever. I'd say he's from out of town, the car is a rental, so we can most likely call some of the companies out at the airport to see if they're missing one. Maybe he's registered at one of the casinos. Hey, you have a camera in your trunk? Take a few shots and we can canvas some of the casinos tonight, you know, stay ahead of the investigation."

"Good idea. I'll get it. Roll the edge of the blanket and tuck it under his head. I'll get a better angle that way."

"How's that? Go ahead, get a good head shot real close. The police photographer will make us copies to take with us. But first, we need to write up the incident and leave it on the chief's desk."

The cop leaned down, tucked the corner of the blanket under Guyler's head and said, "Could you give us a smile there, handsome?"

A low, guttural groan emerged from deep in Greg's chest.

****

"I'll be home Monday. I was thinking you should make an offer right away. We need those two acres to expand and now that I have some cash to invest, well, maybe you could get something in writing. When did you say the For Sale sign went up?"

"About two hours ago. Johnson Realty has the listing. I went out and talked to the agent as he was planting the sign."

"Good work, Jonathan. What did he tell you? I think Johnson handles low-end real estate, so maybe we can get a bargain here."

"He said his Broker of Record wants to sell to a married couple only. What do you think?"

"Jonathan."

"You sound edgy, Kat. What's wrong? What happened? Talk to me."

"I'm fine, but I'm wondering about you. Suddenly you can read me. You may have to delve into the game of poker, test your powers of perception. Seriously, the concentration here is intense."

"Okay, no pressure. He said it's on the market for four thousand an acre."

"Offer them six thousand five hundred for the package and tell him to write it up and present it."

"That might do it. The old guy who owned it for decades passed away and his out-of-town daughter wants to dump it. I'm sure she never expected that pile of weeds to bring her such a nice price."

"Oh, and tell him I will have five hundred up front good faith money for him on Monday. That should make it all official and formal."

"Look at you, spending our money like a drunken sailor."

"Thanks, Jon. I really appreciate all your help. You always go that extra mile."

"Anything for you, pretty dancer. If I play my own cards right, I may become a partner in this business some day."

"You are practically there, you know that."

"In every sense of the word?"

"No pressure. I have enough."

"Sure. You concentrate on the big paycheck. I have plans to start working on. By the way, how's the weather in the deep South? It's pretty warm here."

"We haven't been outside much, what with games three times a day, meals, and room rest. The last time I went out with the girls, though, it was raining pretty hard. There was a lot of heat lightning and thunder, too. The safest place is right here in the casino. Everything I need is right at my fingertips."

"Well, try to relax and keep doing what you are doing because it does seem to be working. And Kat, for the record, I do miss you."

"I'll be back on Sunday night, call you Monday morning. Then it's back to the old, one-two-three step, dip, and twirl."

"We are all proud of you, you know. It's not that we didn't think you'd end up on the money tables, it's just so nice to know that you did. There are a lot of well-wishers Kat, and I'm your biggest fan."

"I know. I appreciate it, too. Tell everyone hello and I will see you all real soon."

Chapter 26

The new dealer was a sleek red head with porcelain skin, slender arms, delicate hands and narrow shoulders. Maggie Youngman felt just fine as she peeked at her cards, an Ace of clubs and a king of spades. She threw in a small bet. Shelly Wintergrass tossed in his matching bet on two queens as did Ronnie Hawke on a jack, ten of hearts. The flop gave Ronnie a possible flush with a six and eight of hearts and a king of diamonds for Maggie who went all in. Shelly folded. The street was a deuce of diamonds. The two ladies sat stone-faced neither one wanting to look at the other. Both knew that this might happen and here it was. Maggie was all in staring down at her Ace, king with another king lying in the flop. Ronnie fingered her jack, ten of hearts and squinted at the two hearts in the flop.

"Here we go, Maggie. Whatever will be, right?"

Maggie pursed her lips and nodded to Ronnie. The dealer's delicate hand slowly turned over the river card, a nine of hearts. Maggie rose and hugged Ronnie warmly and whispered, "Make it a good payday, girl."

****

Kat stirred her coffee. The girls ate their dinner leisurely, discussing the moves of the other players and commiserating with a surprisingly up-beat Maggie.

"You know, Mag, I'd say I was sorry, but you know how the game goes. I just wish it wasn't you. If I had to bet on the three of us, my money would have gone on you to take it all. It was like you were destined to win your first formal tournament."

"Oh, Ronnie, don't apologize, please. I just couldn't read you and that's all there was to it. We always said this time would come and we would have to deal with it. I'm okay. After all, I'll be taking a part of your winnings as per that dark agreement we made, remember?"

"What are your plans now? We never talked about the end of all this, yet here it is." She buttered a piece of crusty bread and looked from Ronnie to Maggie.

"I, for one, will hang around until the bitter end. I spoke to my mom this morning. She doesn't expect me to come home until the tournament is over, so, I'm officially on vacation." Maggie looked relaxed, free of tension.

"Like you said, you need your cut, too."

"I hope one of us takes the first spot."

"It's three hundred and fifty thousand, a nice sum I'd say."

"We'll end up with a nice pile."

The three raised their glasses. Maggie said, "A wise man once said, 'I'll drink to that.' A really stupid one said, 'I don't drink to anything.' Me? I'll drink with the wise man."

"I think Jonathan has me spoiled. He's done such a great job with the studio, I think I'll use a small part of my purse to enter another tournament in the Fall."

"Well now that I've finished in the top tier of players, I will have a reputation to uphold around my precinct. I'm with you, Kat. I'll be watching for an interesting second tournament, too. How about you, Maggie?"

Maggie didn't answer. She was looking over Kat's shoulder to the casino perimeter, the walkway around the gambling floor. Passing slowly through the crowd, she could see the upper bodies of two policemen. One looked too young to be in uniform, the other was heavy, red- faced and tall. They both wore hats with shiny visors trimmed with gold braid. Her eyes were wide with apprehension.

"Uh-oh. Don't be obvious, but look over there, on the perimeter. Do you see what I see?"

Kat turned. "Oh my God. I do not like this. Not at all. Where are they headed, do you suppose?"

"Now listen, you two. We can't afford any of that. Not when we're this close to a brilliant finish. They are here to canvas the desk, the security and so on to see if the picture they have in that manila envelope is anyone they can recognize. Let me get with the crowd to see where they are going and what they find out." She left the table and walked carefully into the passing flow of people.

"I wish I was more like Ronnie. She is so together. If those cops came in here I think I would have fainted dead away."

"No you wouldn't, Kat. You're the strong one. You'd look at the picture, remember how that slime treated us, and tell the cops you never saw that poor man before. How awful for him. Is he all right? And then you'd go back to slicing your fried chicken."

"Hey. After I saw you in action in a muddy field in the rain, lightning and thunder, I have every confidence in your ability to hold steady. So, I guess Ronnie is right. We can do this and we will. He's probably in the hospital, all banged up from that ride down the ditch and when he wakes up, he will belong to the police until they can charge him and sort things out."

Maggie waved at the waitress who was pouring coffees. "You ladies need a refill?"

"Yes, please. This one, too. She's coming right back." Maggie pointed to Ronnie's empty cup.

"I wish I could see the picture. They probably took it right after the tow brought the car to the top. He must have looked awful."

"And more importantly, not at all like himself. With all the scrapes, I'm sure there were more than a few, and Ronnie's barbering technique, he probably looks like a freak."

"Here she comes."

Ronnie settled herself into her chair, picked up her fresh coffee, looked over at her two compadres and smiled."

"Well, tell us. What did you find out? Who did they go to? Are they still here?"

She put her cup down carefully. "First they went to registration. Two of the girls there looked at the picture. I pretended that I was in line behind an elderly couple. I did catch a quick glimpse of the picture and believe me, that does not look at all like our tormentor. He looks tormented himself. I almost feel sorry for him. Almost. They left the desk and went to the poker room.

The one registration clerk pointed in that direction and along they went. I did not go in since it was pretty empty, but Mr. Grady was at a table doing paper work. They showed him the picture and he really took his time with it. But in the end, he shook his head negatively. He made gestures on his head, like he was spiking his hair, then he passed his hand over his eyes and shook his head no again. Then they headed to the security office, but on the way Butch Lanza intercepted them. They shook hands all around, Butch spoke with them, then looked at the picture and reacted pretty much the way Grady did. He shrugged his shoulders and the cops were on their way. Believe me, after three more casinos, they'll head back to the cop shop and pick up another case. This one will lay on a desk up against a radiator and be forgotten."

"I hope you're right. Well, we're too close to the end to worry about all this now. Let's have the nightmares when it's all over."

"Easy for you to say, Maggie. You're done."

"Don't rub it in. I'm going to be sitting there in the dark rooting for both of you to hit it big for all of us." She looked up, her gaze behind the other two ladies. "Oh, hi, Butch."

He sat next to Ronnie. "You said you wouldn't do anything rash. That guy is not recognizable. I hope all the bumps and bruises are from the spill down the hill."

"We didn't beat him up, if that's what you mean. The only thing I did was trim his hair and eyebrows so a picture would slow the process down long enough for us to get out of here without any more incidents."

"Well, I must say, you did a bang-up job. Nobody claimed him. The police said that he's in the hospital with a concussion, broken nose, and a few bone chips around his eye. He's going to need some surgery, but, according to the doctors, he's going to be all right. Without identification, he's going to be a real headache for the police when he's released from the hospital. They'll keep him in lock-up so they can charge him but that's going to take some time. One cop said something about getting a VIN number from the vehicle, but Moe is closed until Monday. You gals will be heading for the hills after that last hand, so I suppose you're home free.

Kat said, "We wouldn't have been able to pull this off without your help and I for one would like to thank you."

"I did nothing. I knew nothing about it and I was here at my job the whole evening. You need to understand that. What you did you did on your own. Secretly, I admire your guts, but I will never say that. But, a word of advice, next time something like this happens, have a sit-down with the casino security head, or the CEO, and hammer it out that way. I know you felt you needed to do this on your own because of your image with the other players and Guyler is the type of guy who would use your complaining against you, make it look like you were all over-reacting, but try the other way, too."

"We had to do it this way, Butch. He was out of control. Hopefully there won't be a next time. Most of the men at the tables were gentlemen. He was just a rotten apple."

"Well, you certainly did a job on him. I believe that if he is ever in another tournament, he will be there to play cards and nothing else, even if there's a baboon at the table. Hey, Maggie, too bad about getting knocked out, but, it's a nice payday, right?"

"That it is. That it is. It doesn't get any better than this trip to Tunica. I, for one, will never forget it. I gained so much experience here. I will always feel confident at the tables now."

He rose. "Good luck to you two. I sincerely hope that one of you makes it to the very top. You're close, make a run for it."

Ronnie looked at him warmly. "You've been great, Butch. My words to Officer Marsh will be glowing so much your ears will be red."

"You leave me and my body parts alone, hear?

Kat put up her hand. "I'm going to have a t-shirt made with a saying on it. I had a barrel of fun in Tunica."

"Or," Maggie chimed in, "how about, 'I had a muddy time in Mississippi.'"

Butch walked away from the table shaking his head.

Sipping her coffee, Kat pushed her blonde hair back. "Well, I am glad that little scene is over. I admit, for a while there, I thought we were dead."

"Me too. But I do feel a whole lot better now. Actually, I feel like a new person. You were talking about entering another tournament before. I just won a hundred and fifty thousand dollars, I have a good job and a nice home. I've been on the straight and narrow all my

life so I've been thinking of hitting the tournament trail for a while, too. We can make a whole lot of extra money just for doing what we enjoy. Not too many people can say that. Look what we're taking home from this tournament. We'd be foolish not to take advantage."
    Ronnie smiled at Maggie. "You know, you're a different person, Maggie. You really pulled your weight when it counted. And look at all the fun we had."

****

    "I got out of the hospital yesterday. I'm fine. All the swelling is gone and the doc said I'd be able to play in this year's softball game."
    "Cops against commissioners. Some rivalry. Aren't you guys just a little bit ashamed of yourselves?"
    "Hey, they beat us two years ago."
    "So, no doughnuts for a month?"
    "Something like that. How are you? I don't mean at the tables, I mean, you, how are you?
    Ronnie took a moment, a deep breath. "Sure, I miss the old crowd, but it's pretty exciting here."
    "The local channel shows bits of the tournament. You look pretty intimidating, like you do at the Ram when we play. We all knew you'd finish up pretty high, but you are the man, you know."
    "I am just a poker player and a female one, make no mistake. It's just that the other players are getting easier for me to read. Thanks for all that practice."
    "Well, all you gals are doing fine. Even that Maggie, she got a nice payday. More than I make in about three years of screwing around with slime bags."

"Poor baby. If it makes you feel any better, we ran into a few low-lifes, too."

"Rotten losers, I guess. Like Officer Lou."

"Hey, lay off. If it weren't for Marsh I wouldn't be here. Ringer told me that Lou's wife has a back problem. You know about that?"

"Sure. She had a car accident at a light. A guy t-boned her. She was in quite a few hospitals. Now she's pretty much in a wheelchair all the time. She works, though. She's a paralegal with Brown and Gibson law offices.

"I was thinking. We had a victim that Ringer thought was killed by a fall because of what looked like trauma to the vertebrae. To be sure, he called in an orthopedic specialist, a new guy at the hospital, who explained why the bones in the lower back looked so strange. It was a new procedure that he said was working wonders on injured spines. It was a material they used between the discs that eased pain and regenerated the nerves along the spine and down the legs."

"Bet it's expensive. Old Lou is in the same financial boat as all of us."

"I'm sure it's costly, but if it works, maybe Lou could find a way."

"Not at the poker table, the guy stinks."

"Maybe we could have our own tournament. If it's for charity, we shouldn't have a problem setting it up. There are a lot of card players in our precinct, and I'm sure other units would be glad to join in, too. If the prize money was spread out, a lot of players would be motivated to try their luck for a good cause. We could make posters to put up in places like the Ram."

Jim said, "You know, that would work and it would be a lot of fun, too. Let's work on it together, like a project. You did say we, right?"

"We'll talk about it next week. I'm getting pretty excited about it. But, getting back to you, are you finished with the snake snitch?"

He sighed. "I sure am. He got involved in a shoot-out, took two to the head. Damn, he was good, too. I'm going to miss him. What do you think? Will you be home by Monday?"

"Probably."

"Because Doc Ringer was wondering if the last hand will be it or are there some events you need to attend. I guess he's getting a little backed up."

"Oh, Doc Ringer was asking? I spoke with him yesterday so he knows my plans. It's funny but he never mentioned anything about being backed up or suddenly swamped with bodies that need hundreds of tests."

"Okay, okay. I was wondering. Are there any events?" She pictured him holding the phone in the crook of his shoulder, gently twirling the cord around his hand.

"No," she said. "I've gone to the last so-called event. After the end, we settle up, go to our rooms, pack up and head out. I can't believe I'm saying this, but I'm going to miss Tunica. It's a great little place with a lot of cute little back roads, inns, roadhouses and friendly people. But, then there's Wade County waiting for me to try to solve some crimes for you cop types. I'll call you as soon as I get home."

"You promise?"

"Promise." She hung up the phone and stared at it thoughtfully for a long moment realizing that she really did miss old Jim. Now that he had the church situation out of his system, maybe he would change his attitude about her job. Funny, she thought, the dead just don't bother me. It's just another job. She'd have to work a bit at getting him to appreciate what she does.

Chapter 27

The next three hands changed the mood at the table. Suddenly, Erik Schneider, who played passively so far, seemed to come alive. Shelly and Kat both went all in with bluff hands against Schneider's Aces which held. He now was second chip leader to Carruthers.

In a long stare down and heavy betting, Schneider left Carruthers with a short stack which he morosely pushed all in with a bluff hand, a queen and eight of clubs against Erik's two tens. When the street flop was a trip ten for Erik, Frank Carruthers stood as the crowd cheered for him and the remaining two players, Ronnie Hawke and Erik Schneider.

"Well, now. We are left with an unlikely final twosome this year, folks," said the announcer. "Not that they haven't exhibited a lot of raw talent. Lady Hawke has an uncanny ability to know exactly when to fold and when to bid. Seems she can smell a bluff after a few glances and a bat of her eyelashes. And Schneider plays close to the vest. If you noticed, he raises when he has a strong hand, like he doesn't believe in bluffs. These last hands should be as exciting as we've seen in a long time."

The two players shook hands. Ronnie pushed back her cap, Erik sipped from a bottle of water and smiled at her with his blue eyes. He took in the crowd seeming to search the faces, squinting into the deep shadows. Then he smiled again.

Shuffling expertly, the dealer glanced stone-faced at the unlikely pair. He tossed cards at them. They both turned up the corners tentatively.

Ronnie twisted a stray wisp of hair thoughtfully. She was holding a seven of clubs and a three of diamonds. Tossing in her bet, she looked at her cards again instead of at Erik. He pulled his king of diamonds and jack of hearts closer, peeked again and raised. She matched his bet.

The flop was a six of clubs, a deuce of diamonds and a queen of clubs giving Ronnie three clubs. She went all in pretty sure that Erik had nothing. Looking at him more closely, she noted his calm visage, facial muscles relaxed lips partly open, void of tension. When he turned over his king of diamonds and jack of hearts, she realized it could go either way. The turn card gave Erik another jack and Ronnie rose to shake hands and give him a hug while the dealer flipped over the river card, a seven of hearts.

"Congratulations, Erik. You played real well and you were pretty hard to read most of the time," she said.

"You were a challenge the whole time. It's hard for me to play against a lady since all my poker games are stag. But you and your lady pals were delightful and I hope we have a match again sometime."

"We will, I bet. And, second place is not too shabby."

****

Butch stood at the foot of Greg Guyler's hospital bed. The room was dim and smelled of antiseptic. Greg was slanted up on two pillows, his face swollen and red. Mike Rossy and Tom Grady positioned themselves in chairs at the side of the bed. A heavy-set police officer filled the doorway.

"Mr. Guyler, we represent the Double Strike Casino where you were a guest and a member of the annual poker tournament. When the police approached us with your photograph, we failed to identify you." Rossy coughed. "It seems your appearance has been altered in addition to cuts and bruises to your face. Do you have any recollection of what happened to you?"

The officer stepped into the room. "Your rental car was from Liberty, out at the airport. We got your pertinent information from them and they are royally pissed at the condition of that vehicle. They're going to claim nine hundred in damages. I think it should be more. The police department will be slapping you with a bunch of fines like DUI, reckless endangerment, trespassing, driving without a license, no seatbelt, to mention a few. You made quite a mess out there in our quiet countryside."

Greg closed his eyes, raised his hand to his face to once again lightly touch the swellings and bruises.

"I don't know, I don't remember. There was a party for the players someplace, out of the casino. The Double Strike set it up. It was free. I remember a driver, a guy who took me there and dropped me off. All the guys were there. It was cool. But all this other stuff, I don't recall any of it. I wrecked the car? I don't remember driving. I was picked up. Casino people had a party for us. God, what happened to me?"

"Relax," Butch said. "You suffered a trauma but the doctors claim you'll be fine in a few weeks. The Double Strike would like to provide a comp room for you until you straighten things out here in Tunica."

"I appreciate that and I may take you up on it. I'm going to call my sister in Westchester. She'll be here to help me out. I think. She should. I don't think she works. I'll try to get her down here. Yes, I will. She should help me out. I have insurance. She'll bring the paper work." His voice was uneven, fading.

"Mr. Guyler, I'm Tom Grady, the tournament director. When you failed to show, the dealer used your chips for the ante until they ran out, but at that point, you were at a money table. We owe you ten thousand for your finishing position. Your money is being held at the Gaming Commission office. When you're able, you need to stop in, sign some papers, show your identification and the money will be turned over to you. You mentioned insurance, I'm sure that will serve for identification purposes. Sorry you couldn't advance any higher."

Greg opened his good eye. "What are you saying? I won something? No shit. I won a prize? His face contorted into a grotesque smile. "Me? I won something in the poker tournament. I was at a final table. Wait until the old man hears that. Oh, boy. I can't wait to see his face when he hears that." Once again his voice weakened.

"You need to rest now," Butch said. He put his hand on Guyler's shoulder. "If you remember anything at all about your, you know, accident or party, or anything, let us know, will you?"

Greg's head was turned to the pillow. He had fallen asleep, a faint smile on his bruised lips.

The officer walked over to the bed. "You casino guys are being very nice, however, the police department has quite a report on this perp, including drunk driving and driving without a license. He has police responsibilities before he cozies up with you casino people."

Mike Rossy put his hand to his chin, furrowed his brow and looked straight at the policeman.

"Well, the way I see it, Mr. Guyler may have been victimized. Maybe you're investigation is off in the wrong direction."

"What do you mean? The report is a simple account of a drunk driver who ended up in a ditch. He went to a party, had too much to drink and got behind the wheel of a vehicle. It's a no brainer as far as I can see."

"You were the officer at the scene, right?"

"Right. Me and a backup. I investigated the town storage lot that he tore up before he ditched."

"When the car was pulled up," Rossy went on, "What did the other officer report?"

"Well, I read his account and it's pretty clear. He and the tow truck driver dragged the perp from the car...."

"Okay. Right there. What side?"

"What side? Oh. He was jammed against the passenger side door. Hm. Maybe he wasn't driving. I see what you mean."

"Not only that. What about that haircut? I don't think he did that himself. Someone drove him out here, as a prank they cut his hair, stole his wallet and pushed the car over the embankment with him in it."

"But why?" The officer put his hand on the back of his neck. "Think the party just got out of hand?"

"Hold on, officer." Butch pointed. "The Double Strike never hosted a party for the poker players."

Grady agreed. "We offer a dinner for the top five players right after tournament ends. It's held in the penthouse suite on the top floor and it's extremely low key. Believe me, no one walks out of there falling down drunk."

"I've been in security for a long, long time. You know what I think? Old Guyler there either pissed off some mean people or he, unfortunately, fell into the hands of a few of our Tunica street kids. Our boy is a victim who is guilty of drinking too much, passing out and providing some folks with a big laugh. That lot you told us that was so tore up. Doesn't that sound like kids? Bet that's where they cut his hair and took his belongings. He's probably lucky that's all they cut. Yes, our boy is guilty of drinking too much, a common sin in Tunica."

"Yeah. Maybe you're right. Hell, it would save us a lot of paper work if we went with that version."

Butch added, "So maybe you could total up the fine and skip the jail time and we can all move on. I don't mean this as a bribe, but you know the Double Strike is always on board for your fund raisers. I just think we don't need to over react. No one was hurt except Bozo here." He pointed at the sleeping Greg.

The four men stared silently at the bed then snickered softly.

****

"Yes, Sammy. You heard me right. I am in the hospital and I will be here for at least two more days before the doctors release me. Talk to the old man, will you? I need the insurance information. He has me covered at the store."

"What happened? How did you end up in the hospital?"

"I'll tell you when you get here."

"Get there? What do you mean, get there? What about the kids? I'm not getting on any airplane. I don't even believe this phone call. What about my kids?"

"Look, take them over to Gene's. They'll watch the kids. I really need you to come and get me. I understand that I finished with some money, so I'll pay for your flight and all that. But I can't drive myself to the airport, I have no ticket or driver's license or anything and my head is messed up. I have trouble remembering things."

There was a long silence at the other end. Samantha was afraid to fly and Greg knew it, or used to know it.

"What about if Eugene comes to get you?"

"No. You do it. I think everyone is going to rag on me for not finishing the tournament. Dad said I would do something foolish and here I am in the hospital not even sure how I got here. It's no big deal. It took me about an hour or so to go from Westchester Airport to Tunica. The airports are small and easy to get around in, so what's the big deal? Today is Wednesday and the doctor said I could be discharged on Saturday. So leave Saturday morning and we could get a flight late in the day or early evening on Saturday. You'll be home for Sunday with the kids. We're talking a couple of hours, Samantha. Come on."

"I'll see what I can do. If I can't make it, someone will be there to help you on Saturday."

"Try to make it. Otherwise, I don't know what to do. I have no identification, credit cards, license, nothing. I am really stranded."

She hung up wondering what to do. There was no way she was going on an airplane even if it was only for an hour or so. She scrunched up her face deep in thought. Then she picked up the phone.

"Hi. Mrs. Anders?"

"Yes, who is this?"

"I'm Samantha Guyler. My father owns Guyler Furniture and my brother Gregory is Nina's friend."

Oh, yes. The Guylers. Of course. Nina is here for another week before she returns to her position in Nyack."

Sammy rolled her eyes. *What a tight-assed snob. Position, my ass. Nina's a teacher, for God's sake. She's not the Lieutenant Governor of New York.* May I speak with her for a moment, please?"

There was a long pause, then a sigh, then the sound of the phone being placed down on the table. Sammy shook her head.

"Hi, Sammy. Long time. How are you doing?"

"I'm fine. School is a struggle, but I'm getting there, finally."

"Good for you. Hang in there. What can I do for you?"

"It's Greg. He's been hurt. He's in a hospital in Tunica."

"Oh, my God. How badly is he hurt? What happened?"

"It's a concussion, a damaged eye, bruises and all. But the doctors say he'll be okay in time. They're releasing him on Saturday. He needs his insurance papers and some identification. I wonder if you'd go down to Tunica to help him out? It would only be a day and I'll give you a round trip ticket."

Nina hesitated. "What about you? Oh, the kids."

"It's not that. I am deathly afraid to fly. My brother, Gene is too busy at the new store and Dad flat out wouldn't even consider going. You remember how stubborn he is when it comes to Greg. That's why Greg called me. I guess the knock on the head made him forget that I'd never get on a plane."

"Let's see. I'm not due back at school until next weekend. Sure, I'll go. It'll be fun to rag on Greg like the old days. I told him I should go with him as his coach when he first got this hair-brained idea to go to Tunica.

I'll come by on Friday to pick up what he needs from you. Say about two?"

"I'll have it ready for you. Nina, maybe you could skip the teasing. He sounded pretty down. I don't know any of the details of what happened, but maybe he needs some support for a couple of days. Lord knows, Daddy will be right there with his special zingers when Greg gets home. He didn't want Greg to go to Tunica in the first place. He warned him that if there was any trouble he wouldn't become involved in any way, shape or form. He means it, too."

"You're right. As I remember, you and Eugene were the favorites in the family. Your dad always exploded at Greg for playing poker in the house instead of doing homework. I usually left your house feeling like a piece of shit. He was always hard on your brother. Of course, Gregory was not exactly an angel. But, between you and me, Greg was not a very good player. I guess he picked up enough savvy over the years to feel confident enough to enter a tournament, but, still, I bet he was shaky at the tables. I'll assess the situation then decide which direction to take. Don't worry. I can be tactful. I've been teasing him since we were little kids, remember?"

"I remember that you were the only girl he let himself sit with to play poker."

"I had fun with him growing up. We cracked on each other a lot and he treated me like one of the guys, but I felt that one day he might see the light."

"I know. Everybody, including this family, gave Greg a hard time. Dad was the worst, always putting him down about everything. Well, maybe now that Dad has other interests he'll go easier on his number two son."

"My aunt mentioned something about that. So it's true? The lady that does my aunt's hair says that the woman is a bookkeeper."

"She is. And at a competitor's store, Feinstein's Furniture Mart. Dad met her two years ago at a Chamber of Commerce meeting. She's a widow, he's a widower, so there you go. It's funny, though. I found out by accidentally overhearing him on the phone with her. He told me all about it and swore me to secrecy. Eugene doesn't know and neither does Greg. He said it would be bad for business, I don't know how but who am I? I kept the secret and now here you are telling me that half of Westchester knows."

"Just my aunt."

"And her hairdresser. You do the math. How the hell did that stylist find out anyway?"

"Come on, Sammy, you know how. The lady in question has a close friend who has a friend who gets her hair done where my aunt does and that's the ball game. Weren't you about to tell me? You said that now that you're dad has other interests, well naturally I'd wonder what these other interests were and you would tell me. You started and I remembered what my aunt told me and soon we were on the same page. So, that's how it happens. You all should be happy for him. Hey, see you on Friday."

****

Maggie felt conflicted about whether this would be the right time to tell Barry or to wait until she got back to Bristol. After all, she pondered, I just met the man. Maybe nothing would materialize, but in her heart of hearts, she felt it would. Oh yes, it would.

"Hi, Barry. Did you see the big loser on TV?"

"It was on the local channel. Just the part about you walking off with a nice big payday. I'm proud of you, missy. You did well."

"I suppose so. It was a great experience. I bonded with some real players. The other two ladies are now true friends, we had some exciting times together, unforgettable events"

"You have to tell me all about it over dinner when you get back. But what else?"

"You know me so well. Okay. There is a man. He's still in the running at the tables. We've managed to have some meaningful contact. He's a retired attorney from Roanoke. We have plans to get together after this tournament is over. He lost his wife five years ago. He's so pleasant, considerate, and real. He's like you, Barry. Nothing phony, all sincerity."

"Maggie, darling Maggie. You sound smitten through and through. But he's about what, twenty years older than you are? Is that going to be okay?" Barry felt the need to play devil's advocate.

"He has fifteen years on me, but he's in great shape, has a wonderful attitude and a healthy retirement plan, plus no baggage."

"You sound so clinical and so very practical. Anything else?"

She lowered her voice as though she thought someone might be listening. "Yes, there is something else. He really thinks I'm cool. He said he likes the way I play poker, my deliberate bets and my smooth complexion. Honest to God, Barry, when I looked into those blue eyes of his, I melted inside. I think that's why I couldn't focus at the last table. He was trying to encourage me but all I could think of was how neat this all turned out. You need to meet him so I can get your opinion. I know you're going to like him."

"Or maybe you just didn't get the cards you needed when it counted. You know how poker is. You're the one who always told me it was ninety percent luck. But, hey, if he makes you feel this great, go for it. And the next time he's in Bristol, let's do lunch so I can form an opinion of the old geezer."

"But he's my geezer."

****

The lounge was almost empty. A few drinkers at the bar and two or three tables of patrons. The lights were low and background music played softly.

Lena sliced the limes expertly, placed the pieces in a stainless steel container and fit it into an ice holder. She took a lemon from a basket and began to slice.

"Hey, Butch. How goes it? Looks like the ladies fell short once again. Bummer. I really wanted one of them to win this year." She pushed his drink to him.

"Maybe next time. Really they're all winners. Each one finished in the nice money, so, they did well."

"I suppose they did. Oh, did you hear about the player who was beaten and thrown in a ditch?"

"No secrets around here. The cops think it might have been some kids looking for a rush. Actually, his cuts and bruises were from the car accident. Anyway, he's going to be all right. Hopefully, he learned some kind of lesson from all this."

"Well, I heard he won some money." She leaned her arm on the bar. "That should take the edge off, know what I mean?"

"Who knows. Maybe if he was able to stick around for a few more rounds, he might have ended up in the top five."

"By the way, how do you like that drink?"

"What did you do?"

"Nothing. I mixed it myself from scratch. You like?"

"Pretty damn good. But why?"

"You teased me about the drinks, remember? How they all come pre-mixed? So I decided to mix you one the old-fashioned way. But I'm not telling you what I put in it. That's a trade secret."

Butch stared down at the flashing amber liquor. He grinned and looked up at Lena.

"Trade secret, right? And you would never tell, even under threat of torture."

"Never. There's one thing you should know about strong women like me, Butch Lanza. We know how to keep secrets, you know, we can keep the yapper shut when we have to."

"I hear you, Babe. You're a real lady of Tunica, aren't you?"

"Right on." She walked down the bar to a waiting customer. Butch continued to stare at the few drops in the glass bottom.

"I can almost see the secret, almost."

The cubes drifted across the bottom on the thin slick of amber. Butch twisted the glass over and over watching the ice and liquor. He smiled broadly and put the glass to his lips, drained it and set it gently back on the coaster.

****

"It's been quite a ride, hasn't it?" Ronnie sipped cola from a can. The girls were packed, paid and relaxing in Maggie's room before leaving the Double Strike for roads that lead home.

"For sure," Maggie agreed. "But before we go, and hear me out, please, because you all know how nervous and flustered I get when there's a problem."

"What now, Maggie? We're home free. Don't go giving me the heebie-jeebies again." Kat stood by the mirror adjusting her pink jacket and tucking blonde strands behind her ears.

"No. Not that. It's something else. You know how we divided the winnings? Well, I've been thinking. I won, by myself, a hundred and fifty thousand. Ronnie, your payoff was three fifty, and Kat, two fifty. With the divvy, Ronnie lost a hundred and I gained a hundred. So we each have two fifty. Let me give you each fifty, that gives me the one fifty I honestly earned, Then you each go to three instead of the two fifty divvy. There. That would make me feel so much better."

"But that wasn't the deal, Maggie." Kat was emphatic.

"That's right. The whole idea was that we're buying each others' trust, remember? Why the change?" Ronnie was rearranging clothes in her suitcase.

"I haven't been a hundred percent with you ladies and now I feel guilty leaving here with this over my head. You see…" She was blushing a scarlet red.

"Oh, no. Did you say anything?"

"Gosh, no. Of course not."

"What then?"

"It's a man. I met a man. We hit it off and now we have plans of our own. Like, you know, a deal." She picked up her suitcase. "He's real sweet and we're practically neighbors. He's a little older, but not that much and he would be a wonderful companion on tournament trips. I never felt so comfortable with anyone and I'm sure he feels comfortable with me. Well, as a matter of fact, I know he does. We just clicked. I can't explain it, but it did happen and I'm so happy I could bust."

Kat began to giggle as Ronnie joined in. They squealed simultaneously, "Erik?"

Maggie slowly shook her head yes as she raised her brows, smiled and shrugged.

"I often wondered, you know, how and when and what if." She walked to the window and looked down at the movement of people below. "When I looked into Erik's blue eyes, I was able to push all doubt off the table. I knew this was the one and any problems could be handled by both of us, together, as one. Do you two understand me, because I feel like, a little foolish."

"Wow, Mags," Ronnie's voice was filled with awe. "You're making me feel jealous. I may just take a closer look at old Jimmy's one dimple."

"What she means," added Kat, "is that we're both happy for you. You'll have to keep us posted because you know that poker players just have to know."

"For sure, Maggie. Be sure to let us know how this all turns out." Ronnie pulled aside the curtain and let the sunshine in. "Just do us all a favor and keep our secret safe. You said he's a lawyer. That makes me real nervous knowing how tenacious lawyers can be once they pick up a scent. I'm the last one who would want to put a damper on your enthusiasm, but I can't help it. When it comes to attorneys, they can be like bloodhounds."

"Not Erik. He's retired and extremely happy to be out of the loop. And you both need not worry about me telling him one little thing. After all, I came out of all this looking like a turd, crawling around in the mud and all. Trust me, no way do I want to start a conversation about all that with a man I respect."

"Okay," Kat said. "I think the three of us understand the stakes and we need to trust each other. Ronnie, your Jimmy is a cop and I talk with Jonathon about everything, but this topic will always be off limits. Now, let's get going. We have planes to catch."

Maggie was beaming. "We'll be in a tournament again, I'm sure. I hope it will be the four of us."

"One thing." Ronnie squinted at her. "When? When did all this bonding take place? You were either gambling, eating, or running bare-assed around the countryside. So when?"

Maggie took a last look around the room then stared at the two ladies sheepishly.

"When you were sleeping."

Chapter 28

Nina leaned back against the seat in the prop jet taking her to Tunica. Samantha had all the paperwork in a manila envelope, insurance, birth certificate, a permit-to-carry photo identification, her round trip ticket and five hundred dollars in cash. Sammy even had her boarding pass which she printed off the internet. That covered Nina's overnight bag fee. Pulling the gun permit card from the mix, Nina slipped it into a zippered pocket in her purse. She looked out the little window at the clouds below the plane, white puffs with shades of dark blue. In two hours she'd land in Memphis. She thought about what Sammy told her about Greg's situation and she was doubtful about remaining sympathetic to his plight.

"I know you, Gregory, and I'd bet the farm that you are the cause of your predicament. You just can't play poker without antagonizing someone. But, we'll see."

The taxi cabs were lined up outside the terminal. Nina tossed her bag into the back seat and asked the driver if he knew where the hospital in Tunica was.

"I do. It's about fifteen minutes from here. Nothing serious, I hope."

"Not really. A friend of mine was mugged. They say it was kids on a spree or something. No one seems to know."

"That's usually how it is. You don't hear too much of that any more, though. It used to be pretty bad, but the cops are cracking down a lot these days. The kids have changed, too. Since the casinos were built a lot of money has been donated to the school system so the crime rate really has gone down. But, around the casinos you have folks who drink too much and become easy targets for the bad apples. You know how that is. They'll catch them, I bet."

"So where are the casinos? All I see are forests and farms."

"There's the hospital up ahead and the casinos are a short half mile further on. They're all on the river."

She paid him and walked up the steps to the hospital lobby. It was a little before noon, central time. Nina had gained an hour, but she was a little hungry. The candy striper at the reception desk told her that Greg was on the second floor in Room 214.

"Where is the cafeteria?"

"Oh, it's in the basement. Make a right when you get off the elevator and it's just down the hall."

Nina took the elevator to the second floor.

Standing in the doorway, she looked sadly at the beaten and broken man in the bed in front of her. She put her bag in the corner and walked over to his side.

"Gregory, what the hell did you do?"

"'Shit, Nina. Where's Sammy? What are you doing here, anyway? Come to gloat? I don't need this, not now."

She pulled a chair over and sat beside him. "Look at you. You're a mess. You forgot that your sister is afraid to fly. So she called me and here I am but I'd like to know why. Why did you end up here?"

He didn't answer her, but he didn't take his eyes from her face. His bruised eye was turning a bluish green. The cuts were scabbed over and his eyebrows bristled.

"What happened, Guyler? Did you piss someone off?"

No comment.

"I brought your paper work." She pulled the envelope from her purse, then the permit-to-carry. "I took out this because I figured you were in enough hot water already." He took the card and held it lightly.

"You're right. This identification would not be a good idea. Anyway, the cops got my motor vehicle information from New York. So put this back in your purse." She took it from him.

"This may have been my fault, but I'm not sure. If you keep that yapper shut for five minutes, I'll tell you what I know."

"So go ahead."

He hiked himself up on his elbow. "Things were going okay. Then this guy comes up to me on the casino floor and tells me he's going to drive me to a private party being held outside the casino for the poker players. He said it was a way to keep us relaxed. Then he drops me off where I have a few free drinks. It was a party with, I think, a lot of the guys from the poker tables. Next thing I know, I'm waking up in this bed, a holy mess. Other people told me stuff like I drove drunk, tore up a city lot and drove into a ditch. I do not remember those things."

She stared at his hair. "I wonder why whoever did this cut your hair and eyebrows. It seems like such a silly, petty thing to do."

"The cops think it was kids just screwing around. I was in the wrong place at the wrong time."

"I don't know, Gregory. It doesn't sound like kids to me at all. Kids don't carry scissors around and do this kind of thing unless they're gays on a rampage. That looks personal to me. Like someone is sending you a message that says, there, take that you turd."

"You're not helping, Nina. I do not remember and you're putting shitty images in my head. Go get a bite to eat in the cafeteria. The doc is coming soon and he's going to release me. Then we'll take it from there. Bring me a coffee, okay?"

The young, spectacled doctor stood next to Greg holding a clipboard. He picked up a few pages and scanned as he spoke.

"Everything is in order, Mr. Guyler, including your insurance. I have all your medical records. Take them to your doctor in New York. They cover everything we did since you arrived here. If he has any questions, I put my card in the packet."

"Am I going to be all right?"

"You suffered a trauma, most of it to the head, so it will take time to heal. You'll have a very thin, short scar under your eye where I removed some bone fragments. I'm prescribing an ointment you can use daily to insure an even healing process. Other than that, the swelling will disappear as well as the cuts and bruises. This discoloration will fade in time, too." He gently inspected Greg's face. "You're officially discharged. Just stop at the business counter on your way out. Everything you need will be waiting for you there. Sorry your vacation here in Tunica was spoiled, but I guess this could have happened anywhere."

"I suppose so. Well, thanks, doc. I'll get dressed and get out of your hair now."

"Do you need help? I can have an aide stop in."

"That won't be necessary, Doctor. I'll help him." Nina stood in the doorway holding a cup of coffee in each hand.

"Please let the nurse at the station down the hall know when you're ready so she can take him down in the wheelchair. Very well, then." He shook Greg's hand and left.

Under Nina's arm she squeezed onto a white plastic bag. She set down the coffees on the night stand and held up the bag.

"You're going to love this." She reached into the bag and pulled out a New York Yankee baseball cap. "If I'm going to be seen with you in public, we need to cover that hair."

"Didn't they have the Mets?"

"What difference does it make? I almost bought one with a magnolia on it. I think it's their state flower or something."

"The casino people brought my stuff over. It's in that closet, on the bottom."

"How very nice of them. They probably feel guilty about all this."

"It's not their fault. Hell, they didn't force me to drink."

"Well, somebody did."

"I've been thinking." He sipped his coffee slowly. "This did happen to me once before, at Phillip's party. I feel the same way like I did then. When I woke up on that beach with old Mona screaming in my face, shit, I didn't remember one single thing. If they didn't come clean, hell, they could have stuck to their psycho story and I'd still be in jail rather than sitting here not remembering again."

He looked so sad, so down, Nina put her hand on his arm. "Let's get you dressed and out of here."

"Okay. Then we need to stop at the casino. They have my valuables in the safe."

"Valuables? Like what?"

"There you go again. Can't I have valuables? My watch, cell phone, some money and, by the way, I did win some dough in that tournament. I did make it to a money table. Can you believe that?"

"What did you win? Twenty dollars and a free pass to the spa?"

"How about ten thousand big ones, smart ass? Me, Greg Guyler finishes in the money. Not bad, eh?"

She stared wide-eyed at him. "I'm impressed. I didn't think you could win if you dropped out."

"Shows how much you know. It's a rule, Krepelli. The dealer takes the antes from your stack until all the chips are gone. Then, whatever position you end up in, they pay you the value. Mine paid ten grand.

Imagine where I might have ended up if I could have stayed at the table. Let's go."

"You're one hot cookie. Put on your hat please."

****

"This guy, Mike Rossy, came to see me in the hospital with that Butch. He said I should stop in his office when I get here. He told me to go to the second floor and follow the sign."

They walked across the casino floor, past the poker room where Greg stopped and watched the players hunched over the green felt, dealers shuffling and dealing out cards.

"Let's go, Greg. It's getting pretty late. The elevators are straight ahead."

Butch Lanza kept his eye on the two figures as they strode purposefully toward the elevators. He thought Guyler looked tired, pale and worn out. The lady with him, however, seemed to be in charge. He picked up the in-house phone and hit the button for security.

"Hey, Mike. Butch. Guyler's here, headed for the elevator."

"Okay. I'll get someone to get the stuff from the safe for him. Thanks for the heads up. Is he alone?"

"No, he has a young lady with him. I guess she's the sister. Do me a favor. When you finish with them, tell them to meet me in the lounge."

"Will do."

"Ah, Mr. Guyler. Glad to see you on your feet. Come on in. Sit down." He indicated two chairs across from his desk.

"This is my old friend from Westchester, Nina Krepelli. Nina, meet Mike Rossy."

She leaned across the desk and shook his hand.

"Have you heard anything about how this could have happened to one of your guests?"

"Nina."

"No, Greg. That's all right. It's a fair question. Miss Krepelli, I have looked at every piece of video from that night and I keep coming up empty. If there was someone who invited Greg to a party and drove him there, I can't find it. Maybe he knew where the cameras were, you know, the dead spots on the casino floor. There are a few places which are not in the camera's angles. As far as a casino party, there wasn't one. Mr. Grady, the gentleman in charge of the tournament has a dinner for the final five which is held right here at the Double Strike. After your friend left the casino, there's nothing. Oh, here's your stuff from the safe." He thanked the young lady who handed him a box. "Check it out, then you could sign for it."

Greg took the lid off the box and looked in. He put his watch on, put the bills in his pocket along with his cell phone. "Seems to all be here. Except my wallet which I would have had with me. Shit."

"After you stop off at the Gaming Commission office which is two doors down the hall, please stop at the lounge before you leave. Butch Lanza wants to buy you a drink. He'll be waiting for you."

Nina stopped Greg in the hall before they went into the Gaming Commission office.

"Don't you think they're all being a little too nice? They have guilt written all over their faces."

He sat down on a narrow bench against the wall. "You think maybe they feel bad that this happened here in Tunica at all? It's bad for business. No one in business needs or wants bad publicity."

She looked at him thoughtfully. "You could be right. I suppose it would be negative publicity. You know that from your dad's furniture business, right?"

"Exactly. He's a stickler about all of his workers being on their toes at all times. The customer comes first, he always preaches to us."

"Right. Right. Okay, let's go make your stops."

****

Butch waved them to a table against the wall. "What would you like? Beer, wine, a mixed drink for the young lady?"

"This is a friend of mine from the home town, Nina Krepelli. My sister couldn't make it. Seems like I forgot that she was afraid to fly. Nina, this is Butch Lanza, one of the pit bosses here."

"Very happy to meet you. Greg, you'll be fine. It will all come back. You'll see." He pointed his pudgy finger at Greg as he spoke. "Now, what can I get you?"

Nina put her bag on the end of the table. "I'll have a white wine. He'll have seven-up. He's on medications. Alcohol will knock him on his ass."

Butch laughed, but inside, he froze. He felt that Nina was too close, like she suspected something. He signaled to a waitress who brought a tray of three drinks.

"So, Greg. What's next?"

"We need to stop at the police station to settle with them," Nina said. "Greg was notified that there would be no charges, just fines, which puzzles me since he was acting outside the law. Maybe I just don't understand these casino towns in the south. After the police stop we'll get to the airport and head home."

"You know your room is yours if you want it. Get a good night's sleep before the plane ride. If you need anything, just ask" He handed Greg a voucher. "Here's dinner for two at our restaurant. If you need anything, just see any floor manager and tell him I said it's okay."

"That's extra special nice, Mr. Lanza. Let me ask you a question. The tournament players, are they all gone?"

Butch looked at her over his beer. "All gone. Right after the losers are paid, they leave. There's a dinner for the top five right after the last hand, then they depart. This accident has been explained by the police. Have them go over it with you when you get there. They'll share everything they have with you. What they really need is for Greg to remember something, anything from that night."

"There were some ladies at those final tables. Were they playing that night, you know, at the tables?"

"As far as I know, every player but Greg has been accounted for. Even after play was over for the night, the ladies you asked about were right here before they retired for the night."

"How would you know that?"

He set down his beer and said, "Just a minute." He rose and went to the bar. He returned with Lena. "This is Lena, our master bartender. Lena, the three ladies from the poker tournament, were they here on Monday night after play was over?"

"Yes sir, the same as they've been every night they were here. They always sat at that corner table and talked poker strategy, had two or three drinks, then left."

Nina smiled crookedly. Greg kept his head down, embarrassed by Nina's questioning.

"I don't mean to doubt you, Lena, but you all seem so damn sure about everything, like it's been rehearsed."

"Not really. They had chits for their drinks. I can double check." She went to a box behind the bar, waved Nina over and showed her the three chits, dated and stamped Monday evening from nine to midnight. "See, they were here, as usual. Why are you so curious?"

"Just trying to get answers. See, Lena, someone did that to poor Mr. Guyler and he's a good friend of mine. I don't want to go back home feeling that I didn't ask the right questions and I didn't get answers. I guess there aren't going to be any. But, thanks for the information."

She sat back down heavily and drummed her fingers on the table, clearly agitated.

"Know what I think, Mr. Lanza?"

"Please, call me Butch and I understand your anxiety and frustration. You're like me. You have to know. Do you play poker?"

Greg brightened. "She sure does and she'd give anyone at those tables a run for their money. I've been playing against her all my life and believe me, she's good, for a girl, she's very good."

"That's the problem, then, Nina. It's your need to know that's driving you. But in this case, unless Greg can remember something about that night, then I doubt that we'll ever know what really happened. I'm just sorry it was one of our guests. Everyone here is just trying to make things a little easier for Greg since he suffered such a trauma."

"I really think, Butch, that it just wasn't one of your guests, but maybe three others as well. That haircut isn't something wild kids would do, but maybe three pissed off ladies might. What about it, Greg? Do you remember getting under those gals' skins, enough to make them erase you from the tables?"

Greg frowned and looked at her through his good eye. His face was flushed with embarrassment. "I don't think I did. I may have made a few cracks. You know how I am. I run off at the mouth sometimes. I don't know. Maybe I did."

Butch pointed at Greg. "You look tired, man. Why don't you drink up and get some sleep then get an early start in the morning. I won't be here, so I'll say so-long now. Take care of yourself and it was nice meeting you, Nina."

"Same here, Butch and thanks for everything. Sorry I was such a pest, but, you know how it is."

Later, in the comp room, Nina sat in a Queen Anne chair near the window. Her lean frame seemed to melt into the soft cushions, long legs crossed at the ankles. Greg sat on the edge of the bed next to his bag. He removed his Yankee baseball cap. His shoulders sagged.

"I really am tired. You're right, it's the pills. Think I'll take a shower and hit the bed. It's a king, see?" He patted the bed with his hand. "So one half is yours. You need some rest, too."

She turned sideways in the chair to face him. "I'm right, you know and I think you do remember. But, and I'm also right on the money with this one, you are too ashamed to admit that some ladies did this to you. It's way more macho to let everyone think you were mugged by some red-neck kids. You wouldn't look so good if it was ladies. I know I'm right. They got your ass good and it's because of that big mouth of yours. You just can't play it cool. One of them took the scissors to you and I could almost hear her telling you to take that, you miserable piece of crap. I feel sorry for you, but, you have to consider that maybe you were the cause of this whole mess."

"I told you I can't remember, Krepelli. Now you can accept that, or continue being a pain in the ass, whatever. Since we were kids you have always been the same way, opinionated and superior. So, think what you like. Right now, I'm going to take a shower. I smell like a hospital."

She leaned back and looked out the window listening to the soft splash of the shower. Greg came back in his boxer shorts and white tee. His short black hair didn't look too bad all wet. His bruised eye had a tinge of yellow blended with some blue and green. She smiled at him. He threw back the covers and crawled under the sheets.

"I guess I'm next."

"Hey, Nina," he said. "That was nice of you to come down here to help me out." His voice was muffled by the pillow. "I really appreciate it, you know."

"Yes, I know. What are you going to do, Greg? I mean in the future, down the road. You can't live with your father forever and take all that negative stuff from him. Did you ever think he might act that way for a reason?"

"What kind of reason? You're babbling again and you are giving me a headache with these riddles about ladies and the casino people, and now my dad. What?"

"Then let me be clear. Your father has a girlfriend. I think he'd be happy if you went out on your own. Anyway, it's time. Go live with Sammy, she can use the rent money."

"Me live with Sammy and her two kids? That could never happen. What do you mean, a girlfriend? He doesn't, you're batty, as usual, me live with Sammy. I should move in with your aunt. Who told you he has a girlfriend, anyway?" Greg was agitated. He held onto the bed sheets tightly.

"I didn't mean to upset you, but it's a known fact that your dad has been seeing a lady from White Plains

for two years now. She's a bookkeeper for Feinstein's Furniture."
"Feinstein's Furniture Mart? My father would love to see that store burn down to the ground. He hates Feinstein. They're fierce competitors. So, see, you are so completely wrong. Why do you like to rile me up, Krepelli? You get a charge out of it or something?"
" She pulled a nightie from her overnight bag and closed the bathroom door.
Greg pulled the covers tightly around his shoulders. He analyzed his situation. If this Nina story was true, maybe he should move out, get out of the old man's hair. Hell, if it's true, so what? Shit, he might even enjoy being on his own. He considered which pieces of furniture he'd ask for. He brightened as he remembered delivering a recliner to a customer in Scarsdale who was a long distance trucker.
"I'm not here most of the time but when I am I need a good recliner for the old back, you know."
"Nice place." Greg and the helper set the recliner in front of a television set.
"It's okay. Like I said, I'm not here much. This was my folk's place. There's even a rental out back, three nice rooms and bath over a double garage. Has a nice deck, too. The old lady who lives there is going to be moving soon. She's ready to go. The steps are getting too much for her."
He would try to get that rental, get out of the old homestead already.
Smelling fresh from the shower, Nina slipped into her side of the king-sized bed.

"Greg?" she whispered. "Did you mean what you said about me playing poker? You know, that stuff you told Butch Lanza?"

Greg breathed deeply, a soft snore escaping his mouth.

"Just like you, you big jerk. A big chance in front of you, a time to go all in and there you are, fast asleep."

Downstairs on the casino floor, slot aisles were sparse with players at this late hour. Butch Lanza walked slowly across the floor to the lounge. Lena was wiping the bar, getting ready to leave, her shift coming to an end.

"Hey, Butch. The usual?"

"Sure, Babe. One for the road."

She pushed his drink over to him and poured one for herself.

"My night is over. We were pretty busy today. How about you? The blackjack crowd keep you on your toes?"

"It wasn't too bad. We mostly had the players who know what they're doing. It's the beginners that need all the coddling. What did you think of our visit from that beat-up poker player and his woman?"

"He was pretty battered. Why was she so interested in the other poker players, especially the three gals? She can't really be serious about those three doing a job like that on a fellow player, can she?"

"I doubt it. I think she's just looking for answers that aren't there. Hell, you even showed her that the ladies were here and she still didn't buy it. I think she just doesn't want to leave here without any resolution."

"Well, if she doesn't believe us or the cops, only her boyfriend can clear it up for her. Maybe some day when all this settles down, he'll remember it all for her."

"You're probably right. Or maybe he'll never remember. He more than likely has it all buried deep in his system somewhere. Oh, well, I'm out of here. See you tomorrow."

"Good night, Butch. Say hello to the Mrs. for me."

"I'll do that. I told her about the drink you made from scratch. She wants to come in to sample it."

"That was the only one I ever did. She'll have to drink what you're drinking because that's the only one I know how to make. Be sure to tell her that so she doesn't come in here asking for a Tia Maria or some exotic one like that. Then it's the packet of stuff thrown in a shaker of soda and ice."

"I'll tell her. We have to be careful of the packets you gals throw into the shaker, right?"

"Take it easy, Butch."

He passed the poker room and stood in the doorway listening to the comments from the few tables occupied by the all-nighters. Some were coarse, others simply stared thoughtfully, and still others laughed out loud at the flops. There were no females present. Here and there he heard some curses and wise cracks. This activity was all acceptable, but he wondered if the language would change if a lady sat at one of the tables. He felt it would. But should it? Is it really a man's game after all? Maybe, he thought, Guyler was justified in trying to discourage the ladies from what he felt was his territory. Maybe the girls did overreact by taking matters so drastically into their own hands. He shrugged, watched a few more hands and headed for the lobby and the main door.

Chapter 29

Dr. Ringer hunched over his desk, his long legs twisted around the wheeled spokes of the chair. Ronnie watched him from the doorway. She placed a pen in the breast pocket of her white lab coat and stepped inside.

"I have the results of that blood work, Dr. Ringer."

"Oh, yes. What did you find? He removed his glasses and rubbed his eyes tiredly.

"It was murder for nothing. She was poisoned all right, just as you suspected. But, it's sad, she was dying of liver disease. Our victim would have been dead in a few months anyway." She handed him the printout.

"Get all the reports on her you came up with and we'll get it over to the police. Just between us, I think the husband will be going to jail."

"I agree. The only good thing about it is that he put the woman out of her misery. Let's not repeat that, though."

He put the reports in an envelope and leaned back. "No. We don't need to give a murderer an edge he doesn't deserve. We simply report our findings and then let the police sort it all out."

"Right. I believe they'll find a big insurance policy, or a girlfriend he has been hiding, or some such motive. It's still technically murder and he will have to pay."

"Ronnie, I'm probably going to retire at the end of this year. The Mrs. and I are both worn down. We're moving to Jacksonville, Florida."

"To your condo? I know you both love it there, but will it be enough for you? You need to keep busy, Sir. We both know that. I'm not surprised at your announcement. We all have been expecting it. You are going to be missed."

"The condo is ideal for us now. And I will keep busy with some consulting I agreed to do with the forensic unit near us. You remember the couple we visit whenever we're there. He runs the unit and calls me from time to time when he has a challenging case. So I'll be a part time consultant for him." He hesitated, looking thoughtfully over at Ronnie. "I wish you were taking over as M.E. but I respect your decision to remain in the lab. Your work there is always right on target. You have come a long way from that alley, Ronnie, and I'm proud of you"

"Thank you, Dr. Ringer. None of this could have happened to me if it weren't for your guidance and encouragement. I do love my work and my life. My vacations give me the time to travel to the poker tournaments, and then, old Jimmy, he's high maintenance, you know."

"Why don't you two become legal already?" He smiled at her over his glasses.

"Maybe. One day in the future. But I'd have to sacrifice a lot. This job, for example. He doesn't like that I work around bodies. Then there's the poker. He doesn't mind the charity stuff around here, but I know he'd begin to object to my trips to tournaments. Until he comes to his senses, we'll just go on the way we are."

"In my day it was called shacking up and it was frowned upon by genteel folks." His phone rang.

"That was the receptionist downstairs. You have company. I'm finally going to meet your poker buddy."

"Oh. They're early. I'll take them on a tour of the new facility and stop by to introduce you. You'll like Maggie."

In the lobby, Erik Schneider and Maggie sat on the edge of their chairs. Outside, traffic moved slowly through the small community. Ronnie walked quickly to them. Maggie rose and the ladies hugged. Ronnie held Maggie at arm's length.

"Look at you, Mags. You look like a model."

Erik beamed.

"Stop it, Ronnie. You look like a doctor in that white coat. It's been a while. You doing okay?"

Ronnie put her hands in her pockets. "Sure. I'm doing real fine. How do you like our new building?"

"It's so big compared to the one in back of that parking lot."

"I know. We love it here. There's so much room and my lab is filled with the latest forensic toys. I know you're not interested but at least act impressed when I show them off to you. Come on, I'll give you a tour."

Erik said, "It's an extremely professional looking structure. I like the white concrete. But it seems too much for this small town, doesn't it? Did anyone object to the project? Quiet communities usually like to stay that way."

"When the plans were presented to the town council, they jumped on it because with three stories to fill, there would be a need or workers and jobs around here are scarce. The M.E. and the Wade County Forensics department hired cafeteria workers, maintenance, technicians, heating and air people, secretaries, all the usual folks that keep a building running smoothly. And, yes, this is a quiet community, but our purpose here is to deal with bodies, so we are quiet, too."

"I see your point." They followed Ronnie as she proudly explained areas of interest. At the M.E.'s door she knocked softly and pushed it open.

"Dr. Ringer? May we come in?"

He walked over to the threesome. "Of course. Hello, Maggie. We finally meet. Sorry I missed you at the old office, but my wife needs me often. Here, sit. Try out our new furniture. You must be Erik." The men shook hands. Ringer sat on the edge of his over-sized desk. "Ronnie tells me you're a retired attorney. What sort of law did you practice?"

"Lots of local stuff, mortgages, divorces, custody settlements, some patent action. Nothing that needed the services of the forensic folks." Erik spoke easily. The two men hit it off.

"Patents? It must be extremely interesting to be in on the launch of a new product. What's involved in obtaining a patent?"

The men warmed to the subject. Ronnie leaned her head toward the door. Maggie left her chair and joined Ronnie. The women left the room.

"Cafeteria?"

"Let's go."

Over cups of coffee, the ladies caught up on some personal news. Maggie stirred her coffee and cocked her head at Ronnie.

"You missed a really neat wedding."

"How did she look?"

"Spectacular. Instead of white, she wore soft pink, a knee-length pouf with a short pink veil with tiny white beads and flowers. Jonathon wore a white suit with a pink tie. He looked so handsome I couldn't take my eyes off him. They make a fine couple. She's not showing too much yet and the dress flattered her figure. But she has so much going for her, those long legs, the blonde hair, and the way she moves, so gracefully, took away from the little belly bump. The reception was in their new dance studio addition and it was great, good food, wonderful music and of course, the dancing was superb. We both wished you could have been there."

"Me too. Jimmy was on a case and our team had to get involved big time. There was no way I could leave the lab until all the tests were done and analyzed. Believe me, I'd rather be at the reunion of the three witches. I spoke with Kat the night before the wedding and wished her well. I'm really happy for them. They both are ecstatic about becoming parents. She always spoke about how much she relied on her Jonathon. We agreed on a mini-vacation early next year. It would be nice for the four of us to get together and do our thing. What else? You and Erik?"

"Pretty good. He's so easy going. There are never any problems like I told you when we were in Tunica. He takes everything in stride. We've played poker in Biloxi,

Mississippi, Covington, Kentucky, Atlantic City, New Jersey, some tournaments in California and, of course, Las Vegas. I use up all my vacation time these days, not like when I was fresh out of technical school and needed to impress my boss by never taking any time off. I lost a lot of vacation days just to prove I was a loyal worker."

"But you love your job, right?"

"Not as much as you do. To tell the truth, Erik wants me to retire. With his income from his retirement accounts plus what we both make on tournaments, I might just call it quits."

"I'll be damned. You've come a long way from Tunica, Mags. In all your travels, have you ever come across you know who?"

Maggie looked left and right conspiratorially, then leaned closer. "No, but when were in Tunica last year, Butch Lanza had dinner with us. He asked about you, by the way. He said they had a tournament there earlier in the year and some of the old players were there, like that fireman, Carruthers, and Shelly Wintergrass, remember them?"

"Yes, I do. Wintergrass was good, but he always looked to the left when he had a bluff hand."

"That's him. Butch also said that Greg Guyler was there. Erik said he was surprised that Guyler would come back to Tunica at all after he was mugged there. Butch asked me if I remembered him and I said his name was familiar, but I couldn't place him. Good acting, right?"

Ronnie shrugged her shoulders. "It's what we do. Was he alone?"

"Get this. Butch said he was with a girl and they seemed pretty tight. She was in the tournament, too and finished four spots ahead of him. They both got a money prize but what surprised me was Butch said Greg didn't seem to mind that she did better than he did."

"Maybe," Ronnie said, "just maybe, he grew up and discovered what girls are really for."

"You think we might have had a little something to do with that transformation? You know, wouldn't it be nice if all that banging around knocked some sense into his miserable little head?"

"Let's leave it at that. Somebody needed to do it for him, why not us? It certainly made our little trip to Tunica unforgettable."

"I agree. We worked damn hard for that boy and after what Butch told me, we did pretty well."

"Remember when you said that we should keep our secret until it was time to tell our grandchildren bedtime stories? Maybe we could push it up a generation and have Kat tell her little one some evening before night-night."

Ronnie said, "We would have to be there to hear it, though. What a story that would be."

The ladies raised their cups and sipped their coffees.

Other books by Dee Alessandra:

Romans' Way

Goldkeepers

North Shore Rhapsody

Valeri Feder

Smart Eyes of Poker

OperationAbout Face

Dee's books can be found on Amazon.com or ask for them at your favorite bookseller.

Made in the USA
Charleston, SC
06 November 2010